LATCHKEY HIGHWAY

for all the creative escapees

LATCHKEY HIGHWAY

a novel

C.L. Herridge

Printed in the United States of America

First Printing, 2017

ISBN-13: 978-0692939260

Images courtesy of Pexels.com
Design by GinaFoxDesign.com

Chapter One:
College, Cooking & Cults

There's a sign on Interstate five at the crossing from California into Oregon that says, 'Welcome To Oregon, Now Go Home.' It's nothing official, just a hand-made sign. Okay, there probably isn't, it's likely an 80s-era anecdote, a myth, like Bigfoot, or ten and a half months of rain. But I still imagine it's there, probably erected by some grumbling native Oregonian, maybe the same one who coined the phrase 'Don't Californicate Oregon.' I get the sarcasm and I love it, but I always get caught up on the word 'Home' when I think about it. Even if that sign never existed, it's real to me.

And I say without hesitation it *is* a myth that the Pacific Northwest is a soggy gloom-land ten months out of the year. Portland has four seasons, just like any other nice place one might call home. But the day I found out I would never go home again, that particular myth held water, so to speak.

Portland, Oregon was blanketed high with a grey-white sheet of Stumptown Elysium. The industrial neighborhood I'd recently joined was quiet apart from the clatter and slam of stack cars rolling and coupling at the rail yard about a mile off, and the occasional delivery truck's back-up alarm. I was preparing for an interview for an entry-level marketing position. I'd been busting my butt as a line cook for three years, and I needed a change. Graphic Design school was an option, but it would mean a stack of student debt. I thought I'd give the employment market one more shot.

I arrived early at the downtown address and plugged about 45 minutes into a parking meter. There were two other candidates in the office's waiting area, dudes both. As the three of us scribbled, I realized the end table was filled with hardbound books, but all the same title; Scientology. I signed and dated the sheets on my clipboard attesting to my honesty and returned it to the receptionist. I sat back down and wondered if there was a bookstore in the building.

About twenty minutes after the two guys had disappeared, I was ushered into an oaky corner office and informed that "Jerry" would be right with me. I took a seat in front of Jerry's handsome desk, behind which loomed an eight-foot-tall bookcase filled top to bottom with the same book.

Jerry and his fabulous smile entered the office and introduced themselves. They slid into the leather executive chair between the oak desk and the monolithic bookcase. As we wrapped up what turned out to be an unusually long interview containing a series of personality questions, he asked me to check in with the receptionist for one last bit of paperwork. I did so, thinking about my parking meter. She asked if I would mind filling out a 'quick questionnaire,' as she shoved a stapled stack into my hand, this time ushering me into the break room, where the two guys were already working on each of their stacks.

The questions were, again, about my personality, how I handle situations, and how others perceive me. How others perceive me?? Is this ever a fair question? Six pages, front and back, full of bubbles to ink in, of the same few queries in different wording. I reached my truck over an hour and a half later to find a soggy parking ticket pasted to the windshield.

I'd lived in an apartment in an industrial, bohemian neighborhood for about a year. The dirt-cheap two-bedroom was situated on the ground floor of a building at least ninety years old. There was a larger apartment above—the kind of place with hardwoods, pocket doors, and built-ins—rented by two women. Our neighbors were a tool & die shop and a fence supply warehouse. There was a door in my living room that went nowhere and the shower and sink were in a different room than the commode, which was in a closet down the hall. It was the coolest place I'd ever lived. I collected my laundry, and checked my voicemail. The receptionist from the consultancy had left a 'Thank you for your time, we'll keep your information on file...' message during the fifteen minutes it took me to drive home.

✦✦✦

I let myself in to my uncle's house to find it the usual squalor. Clothes, magazines, VHS tapes, bottles, dishes, rolls of toilet paper and other things littered the living room and spilled into the hallway. The worn out sofa was clear except for the fortyish white guy stretched out in ripped jeans and a Sinatra t-shirt. I'd seen his flip-flops on the porch but wasn't sure why he'd removed them before entering. There was a path to the kitchen and another one back to the bathroom. Both bedroom doors were shut implying he hadn't been using either room. I said hello and set upon the kitchen path to haul my laundry out to the garage. He greeted me back without looking up.

"Are you still on vacation?" he asked from under his book as I re-entered the cramped living room.

Will was tall, blonde, and handsome—a blue-eyed charmer who often referred to himself as his boss' 'fair-haired boy' in an effort to paint himself as unassuming, reliable, trustworthy. Closer inspection usually revealed that Will often had plans and schemes. He was calculating in his relationships; often working out how to get a particular guy's attention, how to get someone to do what he wanted, how to exact some revenge, or how to get someone to endorse his agenda, whatever it may be. He lived in a different, fantastical world from which he liked to direct and arrange the rest of us for his pleasure. If Will was your fair-haired boy, the wolf wasn't at the door, he was in the kitchen pouring cocktails and asking you about your day.

"Yup, for three more days." I looked around for a suitable spot for the items I'd found in the dryer, unsure of where someone who sleeps on their own couch keeps their clean clothes. "Where should I put these?"

He popped up, dropped his book on the floor and cleared off the two club chairs, finding a misplaced pipe in the process. "Ah! We were looking everywhere for that last night!" I sat in one chair and began folding his t-shirts into the other one.

"I had some friends over last night," he explained. "Ooh, I think there's still a hit in here." He produced a lighter seemingly from nowhere and lit the bowl. It smelled good.

"Should I just leave these here?" I asked about his clean laundry.

"Yeah, that's fine. Thanks." Will wasn't prone to folding laundry. He would have been perfectly happy to upturn the basket onto one of the chairs and choose his shirts and socks each day from the pile. I only folded them because it was something to do.

He offered me dinner. "Are you hungry, I could make some macaroni and cheese with hot dogs?" He ambled into the kitchen to prepare the vittles and I heard him extract a pan from the kitchen sink and run some water.

"Damn it!" he cursed. It sounded like the distress of a man who'd just slopped dishwater on his foot. Or maybe one of the many bowls of green gawd-knows-what former foodstuff had tipped its contents all over the only clean-ish spot on the counter. I didn't go in to find out. The phone pealed from somewhere under the rubble. Will strode in and began lifting papers, magazines, towels and said, "I got it, I know where it is." He located his quarry under a pillow and jabbed an arm to the floor and picked up the handset.

"Hello?"

I stood up and took the second path to the bathroom this time. He was still on the phone when I returned.

"Yeah, we'll fly out as soon as we can. Don't cry, mom." He glanced at me and continued to console my obviously distraught grandmother. "It's okay, we should be able to be there tomorrow. I love you Mom." He threw the handset on the couch and fixed his eyes on me.

"Your mother's dead," he said. A blast of air hit the side of my head and everything was grey for a moment. Then I was trying to breathe and he came in for an awkward hug.

"It's okay," he said. I have to call the airline."

I pulled away to step out the front door where the

light and air could find me. My mom had installed herself in North Beach seventeen years previous, as the Reagan era dawned and the Beat faded, and had since been living in a one-room apartment and screening her calls. On the porch, I held on to the wood support, hiding behind an unkempt rhododendron, looking at, but not seeing the neighbors' houses. The last time I'd seen her was in a hospital in San Francisco about two years before with a severe fever and in a state of delirium as she whispered to me she was sure the bed's rails were full of brandy. I was visiting a familiar stranger that day, and I didn't know what to say to her. Today I felt relief. Will's voice came from the dark side of the screen. "We have a five-twenty a.m. flight." I would have to pack, and leave my key for one of the girls upstairs, and I told him as much in a mumble. Focusing on the task made me feel a little better, like I was in control.

✦✦✦

Back at Will's for the night, I couldn't stay put. He again offered food, but I couldn't stay. His house was about a quarter mile from where I worked. A few blocks over, at a one-story grade school converted to a brewpub and theatre, some of my people would be getting off shift. I walked over in the early evening on a June weekday. The homes in this neighborhood with their roses and rhodies, folk art and wildflowers all looked different. I liked that. By this time tomorrow,

I'd be at Gram's house in a retirement community where the houses all looked exactly alike, and I'd always hated that.

The first time I'd realized my mom drank too much was when I was nine. I came home from school and found her in the bedroom closet, sitting on the floor under the hanging clothes crying.

I turned on a wrong street and realized I was heading away from the pub, then took the first left and righted my trajectory. I could see the parking lot and strode across the street.

As I thought about my mom weeping on the floor of her bedroom closet in the middle of the day, I once again felt relief. I stopped to examine that as if it were an unusual rock I'd found on the ground. I wasn't sure if it was right. I couldn't remember ever hearing anyone else say they were relieved when someone close to them died. I found myself standing in front of a house that looked exactly like Will's and moved on.

I found Petra at one of the bars and commandeered a stool next to her.

"Hey, what are you doing here?" She was spirited.

I hadn't prepared an answer to that question, even thinking for a moment that it was unfair of her to ask. I just wanted it to be a non-thing, I wanted to float around this familiar place without any effort or accountability. I fumbled in my head then managed to scoop it together and act like the friend and co-worked she knew I was.

"Ah, just thought I'd stop in for a drink."

"What have you been doing? Did you go to the beach?" she asked.

"Uh, no." Conversing was a chore. She was my closest friend and I should have been able to confide in her, but it wasn't happening, and it was heavy around my neck. "I had an interview, but I didn't get the job," I told her.

"Oh, that sucks. I'm sorry."

I ordered a pint and she told me about the week's events behind the scenes; so much Sisyphean drama in the kitchen. I pretended to be interested. We drank and a bartender named Bonnie, who was new, refilled us.

"Did I ever tell you," I said, breaking our quiet quaff, "that my mom used to call me 'Bonnie' when I was bad?"

She snorted. "What?! No, you didn't tell me that. But it's funny." She looked at me and grinned. "Like bad Connie becomes Bonnie. Ha!"

I smiled but didn't look back at her. She was right, it was funny. "Yeah, of course this was when I was young, before I was twelve."

"Yeah, you said she disappeared when you were twelve. I remember you telling me that."

"Yeah. Disappeared."

Some of our co-workers filed in and we moved to a small table, a quintet of thirsty cooks and waiters. Our hostess drank lemon drops and talked about her sister's unhappy marriage. I wondered if her sister had the same exotic beauty she had. I wondered this as I open-throated the last half of a pint. She chided a guy nicknamed Deets about his bar-tending skills. Everybody called him "Deets." The reason why is lost to time. The kitchen manager's voice got louder and harsher the more he drank. I polished off ales and doodled. I drew a lanky boy with broad shoulders and a hank of dark hair at his forehead wearing a striped shirt and strumming a guitar. I'd drawn him before, he was a little boy superhero. I'd drawn him once with a backpack and a walking stick at the base of a mountain, and another time spinning the earth on the tip of his finger. *He* had a promising future. *He* had confidence. *He* was ready for any challenge. My left ear began to ring, conveniently squelching the kitchen manager's grating voice. Petra laughed more as our bar tab bloated, and Deets stayed perfectly even, stoic almost. As for me, I was just there taking refuge in the din.

Petra was one of the few good friends I made working in the service industry. People come and go, turnover is high, but some of us stick around and fire up enduring friendships. There's a solidarity among people willing to get their asses handed to them for 45 hours a week and shitty wages.

It was dark when Petra dropped me off. On the way home, I'd told her about my mom, and she said she'd thought there was something wrong. I thanked her with a hug, gripped the bottle of wine they miraculously sold me, and exited her car that was about the size of a roller-skate.

Will was stretched out on the couch again. He looked at me sideways, his eyes clocking me into the kitchen. "We have to get up early, ya' know," he called in to me as I rummaged for a wine key. "I opened the vent in your old room, there's a bed in there."

"You want some wine?" I stepped into the doorway and held the bottle aloft. It felt heavier than any bottle in all the world's wineries.

"No thanks, I'm planning on turning the light out in a few minutes." I ignored his hints. On the back deck I poured a generous amount of pinot noir into a tumbler. I leaned back in a plastic Adirondack chair zipping my sweatshirt tight to protect myself from the rose bushes as they shape-shifted in the dark. The stars drew scimitars and jabbed at my temples. The wine emptied me. I was a small, unnoticed, motherless animal dying in the detritus.

I was cold and being dragged. There was howling. The wail was mine, but my mouth was still. And then I was standing in Will's living room, leaning on the back of the couch, shivering and laboring to open both eyes. "Did I just yell at you?" I asked.

"Don't be a pain in the ass," he said, gathering things together in the half-light. "I'm calling a cab, can you get your shit together in a half hour?"

The brain pain came as I struggled to think about what I needed to do, then gave up. The hangover was the clear and decisive winner. I managed to answer "Yeah, thirty minutes," then forced my feet to swim my swollen head into the bathroom where I threw up.

I found my purse on the back deck next to the empty bottle and spent what seemed like forever re-stuffing it. I rinsed the tumbler in the kitchen sink and chugged tap water from it, dribbling when the cabbie honked. Less than five hours of sleep. We hefted our bags out to the street and I think I blacked out a little between the front door and the departure gate, but I did look forward to sleeping, even upright, for roughly one hour and forty-seven minutes.

Chapter Two:
Back When MTV Played Videos

Mary Watson had a flippy brown wig, round, half-blank eyes, and a wide, toothy smile. She would grin and tip her head kindly to the right, then back to the left as she listened to you, especially if you were twelve years old and describing to her the softness of kittens or Toni Basil's outfit in the "Oh, Mickey" video. Mary and my mom were old friends, the two women raising me and Mary's daughter together since we were babies. It was rumored that Mary and my mom had filled our baby bottles with beer on a particular night so we'd stop wailing and go to sleep, presumably allowing the young moms to stay up late finishing the rest of the beer. It *was* the seventies, after all.

I thought Mary's husband was John Denver. I spent the occasional weekend with the Watsons after my mom left my step-dad when their ten-year marriage couldn't be held together any longer by their mutual penchant for mystery novels. Ellery Queen, Agatha Christie, and Dashiell Hammett just couldn't keep doing all the heavy lifting. We moved in with Gram near

Stanford University, leaving Ted and his enormous book collection spurned in Sacramento.

Linda, my mom, worked the night shift at a hotel near the San Francisco Airport and spent her free time in North Beach as divorce papers and her mail to piled up at Gram's. I rarely saw her. For the first couple months of seventh grade Gram made my meals and shuttled me to and from school.

But for the weekend, it was a good time to be twelve—Mindy Watson and me watching MTV in its infancy, pajama-dancing, making up naughty alternate lyrics to "Shock the Monkey," coaxing the kittens out from under the couch. There was a framed print of a glowing faerie woman and the word "Life" in dreamy lettering hanging in their living room, right above a jukebox with neon bubble tubes.

When my mom failed to pick me up on Sunday morning, we took a day trip to the coast with some of the Watsons' cousins, an affectionate and jovial group who told jokes and rubbed each others' shoulders. When they dropped me off at Gram's, I realized how fun it was to be around people who hugged and smiled as much as they did.

My grandmother's house was neat and orderly, and I was not. I'd found a paint-by-numbers set in a closet in after we moved in, and worked on it for hours one day. I didn't get paint on the carpet, by some miracle, but my hands and shirt were a mess and Gram was livid when she found me.

That Sunday night it was just me and Gram. I told her about the trip to the beach while she made dinner, and she told me she'd spoken to Ted. I hadn't thought much about him since we'd left, and it made me him. I'd been preoccupied with trying to figure out the new living situation—when I'd be able to spend some time with my mom and how to not upset Gram.

"Connie…" She set plates down and I looked at the food. I kicked my foot up under the table and tapped my shoe on the underside a few times. "Stop that!" she said.

"Connie, do you want to go back and live with Ted again?"

My first thought was of the friends I'd left behind. And though I didn't know how it worked, I assumed if I was back in Sacramento, my mom would eventually come back, too.

Gram tried a different approach. "Don't you want to be with your friends? You can't be happy here. Your mom is never around. Wouldn't you be happier there? Ted says he's fine with it."

"Sure, I guess," I said. I was in no position to disagree with my grandmother.

In bed that night I wondered where my mom was. I thought maybe she was working an extra shift and I hoped she'd be home the next day after school. I wanted to ask her what she thought of our plan. I looked forward to getting back to my old life, though I was worried it might mean being separated from her a little longer than either of us really wanted.

At the first opportunity with all three of us at home, Gram told her of the plans we'd been making. My mom's posture was all wrong. It was the first time I'd seen her in about a week, and she was stiff-like, as if she were on a crowded bus with smelly strangers. Her demeanor got worse from there.

Gram wasn't patient. I didn't realize until that night how angry she was at her daughter, and I had no mechanism for understanding why. She told my mom that she and Ted had already made plans, and as my mom proffered weak protestations, she made it clear that it was a declaration, not a request. The two women sparred and I looked on, baffled.

Gram threw one last jab. "She wants to go. Just ask her," she said, pointing at me.

My mom looked at me, and I was horrified to have been dragged into the fray. Shed never looked at me before the way she did when she asked, "Is this true, Connie?" Do you want to live with Ted."

I was so happy she'd come home, but this was not what I'd expected. I didn't want anyone to be arguing. I wanted to explain. I tried to answer. "Yeah, because—"

"Okay, fine. Fine!" My mom crossed her arms and

shook her head. "Go live with Ted then, I guess."

She cocooned herself in bruised feelings and kept her distance from both of us until Ted picked me up during the Christmas break. She was at work when we loaded my things into his truck and I said goodbye to Gram.

Ted worked in a quarry. His pickup usually contained a hard hat and a pair of heavy gloves, and had a perpetual fine sheen of stone dust on it, especially on the side mirrors. I rubbed my finger across the glass, and the friction of the dust made a nasty dry squeaking sound that gave me a shiver, like fingernails on a chalkboard but worse. I always did it, I couldn't resist.

We stopped for dinner at Uncle Lawrence's house on our way back to the valley. Lawrence lived with his girlfriend and her young son, and over dinner, he told anecdotes about the boy's pre-teen antics that he probably thought were amusing, but seemed to irk the boy, who ate his dinner in silence. It made me uncomfortable, but grateful. I was glad that Ted had always been good-natured, making me and my friends laugh, telling us ghost stories and catching toads with us in the summertime, seeing who could catch the biggest one. One night he grossed us all out by putting one on his tongue, a hit performance for an audience of ten-year-olds.

We watched TV after dinner and planned to spend the night. Ted and Lawrence got on well as brothers-in-law, a teetotalers' fraternity. The TV room had a plush sectional for us to crash on. The family retired and we settled in with our pillows and throw blankets. I flopped down on the shorter end with my head at the crux and my toes pushing on the far arm. Ted positioned himself with his head right by mine. I was comfy-cozy, and I looked forward to continuing seventh grade with my friend Katie after Christmas. I rolled to face the back of the couch and asked Ted to rub my shoulders, remembering the trip to the beach with the Taylors, and promptly fell asleep.

I woke up to a huge, rough hand under my shirt, and a face on mine. He'd pulled me onto my back and was making requests. "Kiss me," he pleaded. He squeezed my breast and I was now fully awake in this nightmare. The horrible hand moved down and I stiffened and rolled back over, scooting my body as far away from him as I could, I was frozen and, I hoped, completely closed off. His hand, thankfully, couldn't reach its destination, instead moving my hair to kiss the back of my neck. My shoulders went up and my arms locked across my chest, I was terrified. He groaned, and I heard him sit up. I couldn't speak or move, I pretended to be asleep, I begged to be anywhere but in my body, anything short of dead. He left the room. I struggled to breathe big but to remain tiny and soul-absent.

The next morning I sat on my half of the bench seat in the truck looking out at the world that contained one less little girl. I was alone. I thought about Katie and looked out the window as he talked about the property where he worked. He said there were owls, jackrabbits, coyotes and feral cats out there. He talked about getting a Christmas tree and I spoke as little as I could. He finally stopped talking and I looked at almond trees and onion fields as they sailed by. We stopped for gas and he bought a huge soda. When he asked me if I wanted some I declined. After a while he broke the silence.

"Do you know why your mom and I split up?" he asked about halfway into the trip.

"No." I didn't know anything about adults or why they do what they do.

"Your mother was doing coke," he said.

It was a crushing indictment of my mother's character. He may as well have said she spent her free time snatching newborns and flinging them into the frigid bay for sport.

"All those trips to the city, she was getting loaded with her friends," he said. "I'm sure she still is."

✦✦✦

Me and Ted settled in at opposite ends of the small house where once had dwelled an average family. I was a regular refugee in my room at the front of the house, under the shade of a large tree, and he spent most of his time in the back porch converted into a family room. I didn't know how to follow his rules because I didn't know what they all were since the night at Lawrence's. And yet, as we went along, there were so many rules. Before that night, my biggest concerns were unicorns, quiz scores, and dodgeball. Before that night, I didn't know what sexuality was. I went back to school and balanced learning with vigilance, constantly preoccupied with keeping him—and pretty much every adult male—at a distance. I had my friends to trust, all just kids themselves.

Katie was the first person I told. In the fortress of my room, during a sleep-over, I just said it. "We spent the night at my uncle's house and I woke up and his hand was on my boob and he was kissing me!" Doctors say 'breasts' and teen boys say 'tits.' Twelve year old girls say 'boobs.' And then I sobbed and she just stared. I didn't bother to set it up, or prepare her, or even ask if I could tell her a secret. I just dropped it on her. Then we never talked about it again.

A neighborhood friend of ours fell in love with a girl from another school; her name was Jules, and we befriended her. Jules had hints of the peculiarities of a girl who'd also been jolted into womanhood. She wasn't blameless like Katie. She seemed to be disagreeably punching through the inbetween, like I was. There in her was a woman/girl in possession of a cool, resilient Eastern European brand of beauty usually reserved for Russian dancers juxtaposed with a collection of Garfield plush toys. She drew jelly hearts on her textbook covers like any other tween girl, but hers looked different; razor-like and lethal. I craved spending time with her, assuming a semi-sycophantic role in our bawdy little one-act and learning from her how to manage being the women we were becoming. We looked forward to Friday nights at the roller rink, but more importantly the time we spent outside the skating rink.

Jules and I were planning our escape and going over our story.

"My mom will never know, as long as we're there before 10:00" She had no fear of lying. "I'll tell her I got a headache from the music, so we came out to wait for her."

The local skating rink was lousy with youths on Friday nights, and it was conveniently situated adjacent to an undeveloped and unlit tract with a few cover shrubs and one enormous oak tree right in the middle of it. The only problem was the rink's door policy. They didn't let us just come and go. Parents trusted the controlled environment, the rink employees were like poorly paid baby sitters, and the parents were satisfied to see their kids come out those doors when they collected them at the end of the night. Inexplicably, our ruse worked on Jules' mom.

"Paul and Tommy just went out to the lot, Tommy has some weed." She explained to me our motivations, which were really hers. Both boys wanted her, in fact every boy we hung out with wanted her. I'd end up in a disinterested conversation or at second base with whichever one lost the draw or was lower in the hierarchy. I didn't care for pot, either. We rolled into the girls' room to change. The music was louder in the girls' bathroom. After ditching the skates, we took advantage of the fact that all the managers on duty that night were male and stepped into a stall for a cigarette. Jules perched on the head to pee and we talked about Tommy, sharing the smoke. After a few minutes we heard a female voice we feared was a concession employee. Jules held the cigarette low between her thighs and we froze, listening, hoping not to get busted. She made a risqué remark about the wisps of smoke and dropped the cigarette in the toilet.

I didn't take as long at the mirror as she did and pushed my way out of the cramped girls' room to wait for Jules by the skate counter. I looked at the door, knowing what it meant if our plan failed. We should have been, at thirteen, grateful to be able to spend hours on Friday nights at the rink, staying out until ten o'clock, and not been so greedy as to shoplift even more freedom by sneaking out. If her mom showed up early and saw us coming up from behind the building, we'd be busted for the justified assumption of much more delinquent behavior than just smoking in the bathroom, and there'd be no more Friday nights at the rink for a while. After about fifteen minutes Jules came, having made up her crystal blue eyes and now-shiny pink lips. She walked straight past me toward the one-way door saying 'good night' to the girl in the booth on the way out. I followed without a word.

Out under the oak tree, I was surprised to find Katie getting stoned with Paul. I hadn't seen her inside all night, I would have noticed her in the rink. She was a medalled competition skater and always owned the oval when she was on it, whether or not she was in a skating dress or street clothes. She must have made arrangements for her brother to pick her up this night.

"Hello ladies." Paul had a nonchalant charm about him, and as I saw him there with Katie, I began to think there was something to the rumors about them. "Tommy went to the store, you guys wanna smoke out?"

"Sure!" Jules stepped up, dropped her duffel bag and propped her left foot on a protruding oak root. She rubbed the hand that had been gripping the bag's strap down her denimed left thigh. She didn't want to lose Paul's attentions to Katie, even though Tommy was her target. Jules was invested in her sexuality, refining the entire package; body, face, voice, manufactured vulnerability. Katie had many of her own charms, but she was more invested in academic achievements. I think Jules couldn't imagine that Paul would make the trade. I liked that there was a chink in Jules' sateen armor. The problem was that Paul ended up looking in my direction a few months later, implying that he was simply making the rounds. Jules lit the pipe Paul handed her.

"What about you?" He nodded toward me.

"No thanks." I looked past him, through the darkness to where I could make out the lights of the intersection and the storefront kitty-corner.

"I told Tommy to get some beer," Katie said.

Paul said, "Oh, yeah. Old Tommy's always good for some beer."

Jules exhaled and said, "I'll bet he's good for more than that," drawing a belly laugh out of Paul. I thought about Jules' mom and how it might go down when she picked us up. I already felt like we were in trouble. I would be grounded because one of them did something with one of those boys. I would be stuck at home with Ted for a week, maybe two. Something crunched and stomped closer to us, and Tommy appeared from out of the darkness with a brown bag under his arm.

"Hey, hey! More girls!" Tommy grinned and he and Paul did some kind of congratulatory handshake. "I should go on a beer run more often." He set the bag down and tore it open, unnecessarily. He was animated as he twisted off a can of beer and handed it to Jules, his eyes all over her. She returned his gaze, pulling the red and white can open and engaging her wrist for a demure swallow. These guys were both in high school, Tommy was the older of the two, a sophomore.

Tommy and Jules cut themselves from the group, he telling short anecdotes in an artificially deepened voice, she giggling and swigging. Off they went, lightly bouncing off each other as they walked, heads down to avoid face-planting in the uneven dirt and grass. Katie and Paul and I stood in the darkness, the two of them continuing the conversation they were having before Jules and I doubled the head count. I felt stupid and superfluous, and I wondered if we would get in trouble. The randy pair were less than a dozen feet away on the other side of the oak's trunk, in a spot obscured by shrubbery. We could hear them, though we pretended not to. There were no words on the wind, no conversation could be made out, only giggles and murmurs layered over the rustling of brush. I reached into the torn bag for another can of beer.

Paul picked this moment to acknowledge my presence. "When are you gonna learn how to roller skate?" I froze in place with a mouth full of cheap beer and a head full of dumbassery. I looked at him blankly just to make sure he was addressing me.

"I tried to teach her," Katie offered. And, indeed, she had tried. But all I could do once the skates were on was scoot myself around that smooth, concrete oval, wobbling and holding onto the rail with both hands. I can't dance, either.

I swallowed and said, "I dunno."

"Ah well, as long as you're having fun, that's what

counts, right?" He chuckled, then fished for acknowledgment, "How's the beer?"

"It's good. Thanks," I confirmed. I didn't know who actually bought it, but since I had nothing else to do, I enjoyed it, gratefully.

He returned to his conversation with Katie, and I took a couple steps away to scan the roller rink parking lot. I knew Jules' mom wasn't due for at least a half an hour, but I still looked for the yellow Volkswagen Beetle. There was a set of taillights in the distance, hovering outside the front doors of the rink, and I panicked, dropping a low-volume F-bomb. My heart beat in my ears and I almost dropped the can when the car pulled away and I saw that it wasn't a VW.

Katie came up behind me and demanded, "What?!" She, too, looked across the parking lot.

"Nothing, I thought it was Jules' mom." I said.

"Oh." Her shoulders relaxed and she regarded me, measuring her scolding, "You scared the hell out of me! I thought it was cops or something." She walked away, back around the tree to where Paul had skulked into the relative darkness, and I wondered if I'd poorly executed my reluctant role of default lookout. Maybe a skilled wing-girl would spot the cops before they were in range and alert the rest of the juvenile delinquents in ample time to dispose of the evidence and disband. I would do a better job next time, I vowed, ascribing myself to this duty in the future.

Footsteps behind me drew my attention away from the parking lot. Jules stepped out of the brush straightening her t-shirt and leaning forward to spit something onto the ground. I thought she was getting sick, but she came over to me, begging a swig of my beer. I handed her the can and she took a big pull of it, swishing and spitting that out, too.

"Thanks," she said, handed it back, and moved off to collect her duffel bag.

✳✳✳

Billy Idol's "White Wedding" was mine and Jules' favorite song in eighth grade. We often spent afternoons at her house before her mom came home from work entertaining the boys in our circle of friends and listening to music on her mom's stereo. Her mom didn't care if we had boys in the house when she wasn't home. Virginities were misplaced, maybe not there, but somewhere.

There were a great many sleep-overs, at my house or Jules', sometimes at Katie's. Out of sheer boredom one night, Jules and I realized we could string the telephone cord under the bathroom door, and even sneak a smoke or two out the bathroom window and with the fan running if we wanted to. I thought it would appear innocent enough and I figured I should let Ted know that the one bathroom would be occupied for a while.

"Can we take a bath?" I interrupted his TV program for his quick consent and he looked at me for a moment before he spoke.

"Me and you?" he asked.

"No! Me and Jules." My visceral reaction to his subtle comment was anger, anger that was quickly quelled by a desire to just get the hell away from him. I always needed to ignore the indignity and get away. Like when he would come right into the bathroom—closed door be damned—when I was getting dressed for school just to ask me what I wanted for lunch. Or the time I came out of my room in my nightshirt, a blanket wrapped around me and he came around the corner and pulled the blanket off me, laughing like it was a game. I always 'survived' these micro-assaults, and frustrating though they were, I really just wanted to forget about them and get on with life. Far as I could tell, there was little else I could do but pretend they didn't happen and hope someday things would be different.

"Oh, fine. I don't care," he said, and Jules and I went about setting up our poor-girls' bathhouse.

The two of us fit in the tub, leaning offset at opposite ends like a yin/yang symbol, soaking our teen frames in the warm water, four bony knees sticking out, talking on the phone and smoking. We took turns chatting with boys who were having sleep-overs of their own, and possibly enjoying a tad more freedom than we girls, reducing nearly every conversation to randy double-speak. The more time I spent with Jules, the less I recognized Katie. By the end of eight grade, I was aware of the contrast between them, a perception that had come a long way. It was Katie who had introduced me to Jules, and I had, at the time, assumed there to be a great deal of commonality between them. But as I got to know Jules, I discovered that she had a wickedness that Katie didn't. If Katie was hometown, Jules was Vegas.

✦✦✦

Katie's parents had a giant RV, and I joined them on the occasional family camping trip in the mountains. I couldn't wait to ride in the RV, and I pictured the two of us holding court at the banquette table, playing cards, waving at other drivers, and devouring graham crackers while the two family Dobermans lounged at our feet.

There was a ranch-turned-campground in the El Dorado National Forest. California's central valley's families converged there to pass days and nights away from their stucco two-stories in tents, tipis, trailers and cabins. Some of the families we knew, and some were strangers. Ted had purchased a membership there, too. They were temporary societies, these short getaways. And it was slightly different each time—three, four, maybe five times a year. Each trip featured at least one unknown family just visible and interesting enough to warrant a speculated narrative.

We kids were allowed to wander the grounds; the ghost town, pool area, riding stables, amphitheater, campground loops, restaurant, even the pub. Our routine was to sign up for afternoon trail rides and do most of our wandering after dark. Katie and I stuck together and left her awful sister to her own devices.

Katie always packed a tent, but played down its importance in the scope of the trip's preparations, saying 'just in case,' reassuring her mom that she and her sister would, naturally, billet together in the RV. Once on site, Katie would work out her reason to erect the tent, something her mom wouldn't fight her on. Maybe she'd produce a book from her pack that she planned to devour in the midnight library, or she'd play act that her sister's blanket made her eyes itch. Mom would be too tired to resist by this time, and each sister would have her own space. On this particular trip, Katie and I would share the tent, but more importantly, we'd roll down the highway in the RV waving to the cars.

At home I gathered my gear, thrilled at the prospect of a whole weekend away from Ted. He would drop me off at Katie's on his way to work, and we loaded my sleeping bag and overnight case in to the truck. As I climbed into the cab from the driver's side door I got a boost from Ted's hand up my thirteen-year-old ass. "Where does the goose fly?!" he shouted, and delivered a grope straight between the cheeks and into my hoo-ha—not even a pleasant way to be touched by someone whom you want to touch you intimately, but a violent and painful shove.

"Ha ha ha!" He chortled at my startled reaction as I sat fast, an effort to keep my butt out of his reach, scowling at him. "Go ahead, scoot on over. Don't want to keep 'em waiting," he said.

I never wanted to come back.

After he drove away, Katie informed me, in her highly organized way, that we wouldn't be riding in the RV. Her dad drove the camper, and her sister had claimed shotgun in the passenger-side captain's chair, and the dogs were to enjoy the cabin ride I'd coveted. Katie and I would ride with her mom. Katie knew I was disappointed, and she needled her mom to buy us lunch. She insisted on pizza, even managing to exclude her dad and sister, pointing out that it would be too cumbersome to maneuver the RV in the pizza restaurant's parking lot and getting her mom to promise to bring them leftovers. I loved Katie for her cunning, and for her loyalty to me.

That night, we were stretched out in her tent, talking about the boy we'd met at the pool. "I wonder if his name is really Scott." I wondered this because she and I were in the habit of giving boys names we'd make up on the fly, usually as we passed the mall food court. I chose Sara on more than one occasion, no "h."

"Yeah," she said. "I'm sure it is." She seemed more

compelled by the disorderliness of her sleeping bag. She smoothed, straightened, scooted, and eventually tucked her glasses in their case with barely a look in my direction.

Finally settled, she said, "He's going on the morning trail ride."

"Are we signed up?" I asked.

"No, we have to get to the stable early." She had everything planned, as usual. "The ride may already be full." She said we needed to get some sleep and she sounded just like her mom.

Early in the morning, we padded to the shower building. Katie's black make-up bag was embroidered with a lime green and gold logo that looked like it came from a high-end department store, though I was sure it was yet another sign of Katie's mom's ability to find good-quality things at thrift-budget prices. Her make-up was tetrissed into the bag. I often looked at her eye shadow, or blender, or other item as she applied each and set it on the edge of the porcelain. I looked at them like they were jewels. I wanted to touch one, or ask if I could use it, but I felt like they were off limits, as if my touching them would upset the universal flow of energy and arrangement of matter. Katie's beauty ritual never deviated.

A pushy, rotund woman hardly five feet tall ushered her daughter into a stall and spat a directive, "Don't you ever talk back to Judson in that way!" The mulleted child pouted and locked the metal door saying nothing.

Katie ignored the woman and her impossibly loud muumuu, repacked her make-up bag, and worked on blow-drying her long, chestnut-brown hair. I was using a curling iron to straighten mine, and having fabulous luck.

The trail ride snaked through the wooded hillside below the ghost town. Nine of us rode single file—different members from different families, the guide pointing out indigenous flora, and Scott riding seemingly stag about two horses ahead of Katie and me in our position at the very rear. We bantered loudly about our friends back in the neighborhood, as well as anything else we could think of, just so Scott wouldn't forget we were there and couldn't ignore us.

After the ride, after adjusting our horses' stirrups and securing the lead to their halter-rings as instructed, we headed back to the camper to change. We'd intended to spend the late morning lounging poolside.

"C'mon." Katie grabbed my arm and veered toward the lower campground, skirting the area where her parents' camper was hooked-up. It didn't take me long to realize why. Scott was about a dozen paces ahead of us. "I want to know where he's camped," she said.

"He's gonna know we're following him." I warned.

"We'll just loop back, like we were going for a walk. It's a free country," she said.

The tipis were huge, so the sites were oversized to accommodate them. Katie and I had stayed in one when we came for a campout with Ted. The two of us had the tipi to ourselves and Ted slept by the fire pit on an old cot. That was a fun trip, though Ted had allotted us much less wandering time. Much less.

I recognized the eight-year-old girl with the unfortunate haircut in one of the sites. She was scratching in the dirt with a stick while an older boy threw unseen things at her, pine needles, maybe. She whipped around and dragged a hand over the back of her hair shouting at him, and an even older boy came out of the tipi doling out discipline.

"Knock it the fuck OFF, Jason!"

"I didn't DO anything!" The boy named Jason ran off to the trail behind the tipi emitting a hoarse wail, and the handsome disciplinarian looked at me, ignoring his little sister. I stopped. His cut-offs bore a half-dollar–sized faded spot at the base of the button fly—denim's denotation of endowment. He strutted toward me.

"Hello. I'm Judd." He had tan legs and his black tank top revealed muscular arms and a bit of a farmer's sunburn.

Katie sidled up, but Judd kept his blue eyes on me.

"I'm Connie," I squeaked, "I saw your sister before." I said in an effort to establish some connection.

He was holding a length of heavy twine, wrapped around each hand with about a foot and a half dangling between and stabilized by his thumbs as if he'd been measuring something. "Ah, she's not really my sister. More like a pet." His good-ole'-boy smile lit me up.

"Where did you see her? What did you catch her doing?" he asked, moving two steps closer to me.

"We should go." Katie said, severing the spell. I looked at her knowing she was right, and I stepped off, almost tripping over nothing.

I flailed my arms checking the dusty ground at my feet. "Gotta go. I'll see you around." When I looked back up at him, he was still smiling.

"Hope so," he said.

I made my legs work again and we continued.

"Did you *see* him?"

"I've seen him here a few times, what did he say his name was?" she asked, as if cataloging the event.

"Judd." I fluttered. "I like him." I looked back, but there was no sign of any of them.

She shrugged, "Yeah, he's okay, I guess." She was walking a little stiff, or maybe it just seemed so by comparison to my vacuous promenade. "We just passed Scott's campsite."

I'd forgotten why we were on that loop. "Really?" I

whirled around to see which one.

"Don't look!" She scolded.

"Oh, sorry."

✦✦✦

The campground's "ghost town" was a row of vintage storefronts. Actually it was the leftover set of a TV Western from the 60s. Just down the hill from that was the riding arena and trail ride staging area. Between them was a set of bleachers built into a gentle slope. That was where we ended up that night; Katie, Scott, and me. He'd attached himself to us that afternoon as we'd sunned ourselves by the pool. She flirted enough for the both of us, every other sentence she uttered had a double meaning. He ate it up.

We sat on the bleachers in the mountain darkness. There was nothing but an empty arena sprawled out in front of us, and woods beyond that. The rest of the campground, all the adults, Katie's bitchy sister, even mullet-girl were all somewhere over the hill behind us. And Judd, too. I sat on Scott's left, Katie on his right and I listened to her talking about horses and such. He redirected the conversation talking about his dad's speedboat, and I occasionally participated by asking a dull question, the answer to which I didn't particularly care about, trying to justify my presence. I was thinking about Judd. I wondered if he'd caught me looking at his shorts. Maybe that was the reason for his wide smile.

Katie giggled and her voice lifted, ending in the word "ram." Her question was obviously a double entendre, whatever it was. The night was momentarily dead quiet and I realized they were kissing. I looked over to confirm and Scott pulled from her and turned to me, leaning in hard and jamming his tongue between my lips. The half-second of awkwardness ceased when I kissed back. I think he kissed me longer than he kissed her. I think. He swung back to her, and at the same time put his left hand on my right thigh as if to keep me in place. I didn't know where his other hand was. I put my hand over his and wanted to push it but didn't know how. I was flushed and suddenly afraid of someone seeing us. More than that, I felt eyes on us; treacherous eyes from the woods that saw how badly I wanted him to kiss me again. I broke our crude trinity in a panic, citing curfew. To my relief, Katie concurred, even though we had almost an hour before we had to be back at the camper. I left the two of them on the bleachers to say goodnight, and waited for her at the unlit edge of the ghost town. I had a not-quite-sick, funky feeling in my gut. She walked up out of the darkness as if we'd done nothing wrong. Walking the trail back to our tent outside the camper, she was super-cool, unlike my flighty performance at the tipis that morning.

We repeated our grooming ritual the following morning and Katie went to have breakfast with Scott before he and his family pulled out. She assumed I'd come along, but I wasn't interested.

I went to the pool despite the cool, cloudy morning. I stretched out in one of the lounge chairs, a sweatshirt and shorts over my swimsuit, and waited for it to warm up enough to swim. I regarded each of the half dozen or so others there one at a time until I figured out what the hell they were individually doing by a swimming pool on such a chilly morning. Two grizzled men were playing a board game, but it wasn't chess. A mother was reading a tabloid in her robe while her toddler son sat at the edge of the kiddie pool, one foot in the water and pulverizing chips at its edge. He looked at her a few times, waiting for his window of opportunity to sweep the chip shrapnel into the water without getting scolded. I swear his mom knew what he was doing, and was just playing his game from behind the rag she was reading. A woman in what looked like an expensive tennis dress stood by one of the gates, gripping a to-go cup of coffee and eyeballing the parking lot.

The sun pushed out from behind a cloud and warmed my face.

I squinted against its glare and stared slack-jawed at a boy intent on something in the shrubbery on the other side of the pool, across a stretch of grass. He was wearing dark blue jeans cut off just above his knees, and no shirt or shoes. He was maybe only a couple years younger than me and cussed at the bushes. I squinted harder and sat up when I realized I was staring agape at Jason, Judd's brother. He caught me eyeballing him and hammed it up. He raised his arms and wiggled grinning between two trimmed boxwoods to retrieve what turned out to be a frisbee.

Emerging from the landscaping, he held it up and shouted, "Hell yeah! It's mine, now." Everyone but Tennis Dress looked at him. I settled back in my chaise, and he seemed disappointed. I caught sight of Tennis Dress exiting, the spring-loaded gate slamming behind her, and I unzipped my sweatshirt.

A splash, a four-second delay, and a voice-cracked screech told me everything I needed to know without looking; Jason had hit the water and was swimming over. Jason wanted attention wherever he could get it.

"Is this yours?" He'd scampered out of the water and was dripping at the foot of my lounge, tambourining the frisbee.

"Nope, not m—"

"You know my brother?" He asked, his voice cracking again.

I blinked at him while I slipped off my sweatshirt to mop the chlorine-water drips off my ankles. He was annoying but cute. He was really cute; freckled with bright green eyes and a tousle of reddish-brown hair; probably tall for his age, scrawny and tan. This boy was also pushy, socially awkward and squirrelly. He had a bad bit of road rash on both knees and down his left calf. He stared.

"I know you know my brother, I saw you talking to him," he insisted.

"I don't know your brother." I was starting to feel kinda squirrelly myself.

"Oh, okay!" Jason chirped, and bounded off.

His departure was a relief, he was an intense character. I took a moment to calculate to what extent I'd lied to him. I did know his brother, after all. Or, at least, I wanted to know his brother. That is to say, I knew who his brother was. It didn't matter much, we were leaving the next day.

It warmed up, and I stayed there by the pool through what I was sure to be the length of Katie's farewell breakfast with Scott. I was plenty comfortable and had no reason to move. The chaise was like a home I thought I would never have. I wondered if I should check in with Katie's parents, and even liked the idea of doing so. I yearned to extend someone the respect due an authority figure.

But I didn't check in with them, mostly to avoid Katie's sister. She'd tried unsuccessfully to rekindle a romance with one of the stable hands, and she was in a foul mood.

Katie joined me on the deck, plopping down on a chaise next to mine and told me about her breakfast date while I half listened. "Your blonde boy-toy was in the dining hall." She concluded her narrative with this bit of information, and I came to attention.

"Was he with his family?" I asked, "Because his brother was out here when I got here."

"It looked like his mom and sister, and I guess maybe another brother were there." She said. "I'm going to change into my bathing suit, you stayin' here?"

"Yeah."

"I'll be right back." She hustled out the gate, and I got up to put my toes in the water.

It was warmer than I'd expected, and the glimmer off the pool's surface was mesmerizing. I pushed my ankles around in the water, sitting on the concrete edge and listening to the din of the growing group of bathers around me. Chip Boy and his mother were gone, and campers in bikinis, tank suits and board shorts had started ambling in and filling chairs. I wanted to talk to Judd one more time before we pulled up stakes. I wondered if Katie and Scott had exchanged numbers. I wondered how I would ask Judd for his.

It wasn't noon yet, but the concrete warmed my butt through my shorts. We'd just read A Tree Grows in Brooklyn in English class. I remembered the author's description of a mother's vigorous scrubbing of the spot where an assailant's penis had touched her teen daughter after an attempted sexual assault. The scrubbing had made the girl's flesh raw, but they still couldn't erase the feeling of filthy betrayal in that one spot. I felt the same way sitting on that warm concrete.

Legs dangling into the blue, I straightened my back, planted my palms on the pool's edge on either side of me, locking my elbows, and hung my head between my shoulders. All I could see were the surface water glimmers, and they were starting to affect my vision. After a while of reverie, I turned my head toward the gate in time to see what I thought was Katie coming back. I was posed like a macabre marionette and imagined slipping forward into the water like something dead. I pulled my gaze back to center, closed my eyes again and breathed deep. The sparkles went black on red behind my eyelids, and I felt I could stretch my back and neck even further. I was an acrobat, or a faerie, or a dragonfly. I was a dolphin or a mer—

"You look silly." Katie's critique of my daydream posture was punctuated by the drop of her towel and lotion on the foot of her chaise. "What are you doing?"

I opened my eyes and slumped. "Nothing." I turned my face away from her and saw Judd in the distance. "Shit!"

"What?" She looked before I could tell her not to. "Oh. Well, you didn't look like a total dork. I just thought you were about to pass out."

"Great." I looked back down at the water and rubbed the heel of my hand over my eye.

"You didn't know he was there?" she asked. "He's staring right at us, should I wave?" She waved.

"Oh my gawd. You're trying to embarrass me to death." I went stiff, but managed to look up in time to see him push his sunglasses on top of his head. She was in a black, halter-strapped one-piece cut high at the thighs, and low in the back. She was thin, but not skinny. I knew she had no plans to go after him, but she looked so damn good. I wore a purple and green, semi-string bikini with cut-offs, and had no plans to take my shorts off. I decided at that moment to forget about him. We'd only be there another day, and even if he had been interested in me, it was probably just to get closer to her. And if that hadn't been the case already, it probably was now. It seemed an impossible task, getting his attentions, and then his number. Being the bitter, put-upon, nerdy friend was much less work. I slinked into the pool just as she was saying something.

"He's kinda ffreeeoooommmyyy."

I stayed under the water for a few minutes, not really caring what she thought, until lack of oxygen piqued my curiosity. Up I popped.

"What?" I asked through the shedding chlorine-water.

She was settling into the chaise, "I said, he's kind of freaky."

I shrugged.

"What, now you're not interested?" she asked.

I gripped the edge with my fingertips and put my feet flat against the wall toward the bottom, stretching my arms and legs, making a 'greater than' symbol with my body. " I dunno, we're leaving tomorrow," I posited, "and I've hardly talked to him." I glanced at him. He was looking in our direction, at me it seemed, but I couldn't be sure. I maintained my newfound disinterest just the same. "What do you mean he's freaky?"

"I don't know..." She looked quickly over at him. He was quite a distance from us—from everyone in fact. There were others in the pool area; around us or at the concession stand, near the wading pool, or sitting on the edge like I had been. Judd was stretched out in a chair that he must have pulled away from an umbrella table and dragged to the farthest end of the pool area. He was in jeans and a muscle shirt, surveying the scene with his back to the hedge. "He's just kinda weird." She was rubbing lotion on her legs. "He's not my type, at all."

I let my feet fall and rested my chin on my hands on the pool edge. "Maybe I'll talk to him," I mumbled, looking at a ladybug.

"You should." She said, adjusting the back tilt of her chaise.

I asked her if she was going to get in the pool and she reminded me that she'd just put on tanning lotion. She also said she probably wouldn't since she was wearing make-up. It wasn't a snooty gesture; her motivations were purely practical. Katie wasn't haughty, nor self-centered. She just didn't have any of that in her. She was practical.

✸✸✸

"I'm gonna have to quit free-basing. Last time I did, I thought up the perfect way to get rid of my mom's husband." Judd smirked, then added, "You have beautiful legs." We sat at a picnic table in front of the ghost town.

Katie, it turned out, truly wasn't interested in him. After hot dogs for dinner at the camper, she and I had gone for a walk, ending up at the ghost town. As we passed the used bookstore heading for the gift shop, our last evening at the campground took a timely turn. I'd stopped, frozen on the boardwalk, half hiding behind and holding onto one of the four-by-four upright beams that supported the overhang above the row of storefronts. I'd stopped to watch Judd walking straight toward me.

"I'll be inside." Katie saw his determined approach and seized the opportunity on my behalf. He walked slightly bow-legged—and bow-armed for that matter, as do guys with big quads.

I was wearing, still, the shorts I'd been swimming in and an oversized sweater. He'd ushered us to the picnic table at the farthest end, in front of a pottery studio, and alongside a cypress hedge.

His comment about my legs embarrassed me. Even so, we huddled in the semi-darkness talking about anything. I told him where I lived and what mall me and Katie hung out at. He told me that two of his siblings were fosters that had been adopted, and that Jason was his real brother. He mentioned that he wasn't "worried about Jason." I didn't know what he meant by that, nor by his remarks about his mother's husband. I didn't know what free-basing was, either, but I thought it had something to do with weed. He told me about a blonde Native American girl who lived up the street from him named Hope. He said she was a good friend of his, and that he'd like me to meet her. I was smitten. He wanted me to meet his friends.

His blue eyes sparked with effortless charm and he swept his blonde hair back with a rough hand to make a fit feather on either side of his head. "You okay?"

"Mmm, I'm cold," was the best I could muster.

Katie came out and stood next to the table. She'd bought a bottle of perfume.

"Hello." Judd said to her in a formal and impatient tone.

"Hi," came her obligatory response. They looked at each other for a moment, then she softened her posture and told me she was going back to the camper to drop off her purchase.

"What are you going to tell your mom about why I'm not with you?"

"I'll tell them you're shopping or something. And that I'm coming back and meet you. It's no biggie, you guys hang out here as long as you want. I'll kill some time. I'll be back." She ambled off and Judd watched her go.

"That chick's none too fond of me," he said when she was out of earshot.

All I could do was look at him and blink a few times. "Nah, she's okay." I reassured. Then I backpedaled. "What d'you mean?"

"Oh, I've seen her here before. She's never been overly friendly toward me." He moved his hand on the table right next to mine, just touching.

I wanted to change the conversation. "Do you like coming here?" As soon as I asked the question, I felt stupid.

"Sure, my dad almost never comes with us." I was confused, and before I could ask him to clarify, he explained, "The guy my mom is married to, he's supposedly my father, but I don't think he really is." His tone was chilly on this declaration, but the movement of his lips heated me up. He grinned. I realized we were the only ones out there aside from the crickets and moths. There seemed to be too much table between us and I stood to walk around, kicking at the gravel and looking at the stars, or at the woods in the dark distance. There were a number of overhead lights, but not above where we were sitting. I loitered a bit, pretending to be restless, or stretching my legs, or some other bullshit, then I settled back down, next to him this time. It was a masterful ploy that hopefully would end in the most possible parts of our bodies touching without actually fucking on a picnic bench.

I thought about Ted many, many miles away, out of range. If he'd been on the trip, and if I'd actually gotten this far out of his sight, he'd have already come stomping around the corner and dragged me away, spitting and howling, and threatening Judd. But he wasn't.

I stood up and took a couple steps away, my back to Judd, looking at the darkened trees, relishing being any distance from Ted, and it occurred to me that I didn't know how old Judd was.

"There's a lot of coyotes around here." He issued the warning close into my ear as he was now standing right behind me, and his hands found my hips. I leaned back into him just enough.

"Coyotes aren't the dangerous ones, are they?" I asked. "Isn't that wolves?"

✦✦✦

The council held in my grandmother's living room that spring was to discuss a change of scenery for me.

Gram, Lawrence and Ted talked about me with mild exasperation as if I wasn't there. Gram planned to help Lawrence buy his first house, and after I finished eighth grade I would move in with him. It was a relief. Only a few more months and I would be back in the family, maybe even get to see my mom. I'd talked to her a few times while I was living with Ted, at Christmas and on my birthday, and I'd been hoping she'd someday come back. She hated Sacramento, but I figured I had a good chance of getting some time with her once I was in San Mateo. I had to make up for hurting her feelings. I was thrilled, I just had to get through the last few months with Ted.

He'd become intensely possessive, twice accusing me of making plans I'd never made. The first time he'd grounded me saying he'd heard me planning to meet 'a boy,' during a phone conversation—a conversation that never took place. The second time, the incident that scared me more than any of the other incidents, was when he sat me down and calmly told me he knew of my plans to run away. I'd had no such plans. He wasn't a drinker, which made these scenes that much more sinister. He wasn't addled. But he'd manufactured justification for keeping me in a little box.

But now I would be able to move on from him. I could get on and forget.

Gram and Lawrence told Ted about their plan, and

he hemmed and hawed before proffering a warning to my uncle. I sat on the floor and listened to the adults talk while I played with my grandmother's cat with my shoelace.

"Connie, are you going to just hide out in your room?" Gram asked. I was drawn into the conversation by an inquisition regarding Ted's apparent biggest complaints about me, the fact that I'd spent two years avoiding him, and that I didn't appreciate him.

"Well?! If you go live with Lawrence, are you going to just hide in your room, like you do to Ted?" She was impatient, asking with an erect right hand if I would be as aloof as my uncle's charge as I had been as Ted's.

"No, I wouldn't do that to Lawrence." I blurted it out. I didn't know my uncle, I didn't know how we would get along, but I fancied it my ticket out of Ted's authority. I would have said anything.

Ted and I drove the two hours back home that night taking Lawrence home on the way. He'd since broken up with his girlfriend and had rented a bachelor's apartment. At his place I went in to retrieve a book he said he'd bought for me at a garage sale. It was a thick, hardcover tome he'd had on the entry table just inside the front door. He held it in both hands against his shirtfront, looked at me, and asked, "So, are you positive you want to come live with me?"

I was befuddled but I answered without hesitation. "Oh yes! Definitely."

He gave me a big hug and said, "Oh good, I'm so glad," and handed me the book. It was an encyclopedia of dog breeds.

✱✱✱

In June I packed up my room and Ted held a massive garage sale. One more night in the mostly empty house and Will and Lawrence would pick me up and Ted would be out of my life. I would live with Lawrence, spend time with mom, go to the same high school she did, maybe see Gram and Auntie Elyse at Christmas, despite the fact that neither of them were big fans of mine. Elyse was petite and pretty, and always put together just so. When I was young, I'd listen as the adults talked and Elyse's quips always made me giggle. But her wit had a cruel edge. More than once I was cut down mid-mirth by an acid-tongued comment reserved just for me. I adored her, and I hoped this would be my opportunity to get her to like me.

I sat in the only chair in the living room while Ted cleared things out of the family room, hauling them out through the garage. I didn't talk to him any more than I had to; I'd answered his questions and more or less kept the peace over the year and a half, and now, as our time came to its close, I had nothing at all to say. But the mood was different now, as he also had nothing to say to me. He passed through the living room and pushed into my room, then into the room next to it, then back through to the dining room and grabbed a stack of papers and a magazine off the end of the kitchen counter. I sighed and looked at my sandals. He strode back out to the family room then turned around in the entryway and said, "Get off your butt and help me!"

Without looking at him I said, "If it'll get me out of here faster," and got up.

The magazine hit the floor near my feet and the papers fluttered after it. It startled me and I looked up at him as he was coming toward me. I tried to get away and fell to my knees and he grabbed my arms. I tried to pull free, and I screamed and started crying. He pushed me down and straddled me and held my arms down.

He screamed in my face, "What the hell did I do that was so bad that you and your mother treat me like this?!"

I turned my face away and he yelled again, "You treat me like an asshole!"

He got off me and scooted away, settling against the wall at the far end of the room. He sighed and ran his fingers through his thick black hair and said, "You know your uncle won't take this crap, right?"

I balled myself up on the floor in the fetal position and refused to make eye contact with him, though I could see him through my hair. He got to his feet and disappeared through the family room and out to the garage. I stayed there on the carpet, afraid to move. I fell asleep and it was dark when I woke up. The porch light was on and shone into the living room. I got up and went to my room. Ted wasn't there when Will and Lawrence arrived in the morning.

✱✱✱

Will and I took our seats near the back of the plane and I got the aisle seat, my favorite. I dug my sketchbook out of my carry-on and looked at the previous night's drawings of the broad-shouldered boy. Sometimes I got his adorable face just right. Will leaned in and looked at the sketch.

"So cute, how old is he?" he asked.

"He's ten, Will," I closed and stowed the sketchbook and stared ahead at the passengers settling in. Will took the window even though it wasn't his assigned seat. He buckled himself in and looked out at the baggage handlers. He said, "you should go to art school," so quietly I barely heard it.

I thought to myself that I probably would. I suddenly couldn't think of a reason not to. His seat's occupant came up the aisle, stopped at our row, looked at him, looked at her boarding pass, then back at him. He moved to the middle seat and apologized graciously to the slight woman who seemed not to speak much English. She slid in and he buckled in next to me saying, "I guess I read it wrong." He hadn't read anything wrong, and we all knew it. I stared ahead.

As we taxied, I leaned over and said, "You know what's funny? I always thought she'd come back. I've been waiting for her to come back, not go away for good."

Will was a guarded man; he was emotional on cue, on his own terms, but this revelation hit him at his core as was evidenced by the tone of his two word answer. "Oh, Connie." I knew him well enough to know I'd gotten to him.

✦✦✦

I stayed at Lawrence's apartment for a couple days, watching TV during the day while he was at work. The house he'd bought was being renovated. My uncle's furnishings and appointments were a full one-eighty departure from Ted's very lived-in household. Lawrence's apartment was like a museum, the rooms breathed austerity. I was afraid to touch anything, but I was also curious about the uncle I'd never known very well.

There wasn't much on TV except I Love Lucy, and not much more in the bachelor's refrigerator. The kitchen looked as though it had never been cooked in. I toasted and buttered a slice of bread, and washed and replaced the knife. It seemed a good idea to not perturb my new host lest he send me back. In front of the TV I perched on the edge of the sofa to take in the social choreography of Lucy and Ricky and their neighbors. Nap time followed. When I woke up, Lawrence was home, and within an hour we were back on the road. He told me I'd be staying at Gram's for the next week until we could move into his house.

We drove down to Gram's in the twilight and I wondered why I had lived the last two years with Ted, and what had changed? Was it something I'd done? I wondered if I would be able to find the sense in any of it, because mostly I wanted to have some kind of control over what happened to me in the future. I looked out the window as if the answers were out on that highway somewhere.

"Are you hungry?" he asked.

"I'm starving, I haven't eaten anything all day."

"You had toast," he said. "You know how I know? The toaster was crooked and there were crumbs in the sink."

I got a nervous chill and didn't know what to say. I was disappointed that I'd screwed up already, but I promised myself I'd do better. I wanted everything to work out, I didn't want to be sent back to Ted.

Over dinner, Lawrence talked about the work being done on the house, but I only cared about one detail: the fact that the bungalow backed up to the stable yard of a race track. I'd be able to peek over the fence and see the beautiful horses. I'd hear their clomps and snorts, and smell their musk—they were *that* close. I could study them as they exercised, and sketch them.

They said Will would occupy the guest cottage in the back yard. I was happy. I wanted to take care of my uncles, and I wanted to spend some time with my mom. I had grand plans, though it felt odd that things were working out so well. The previous unhappiness seemed so unnecessary.

Chapter Three: Goody Two-Shoes

A red-haired girl with pouty lips and plentiful curves in broken-in Levi's took the desk next to me in ninth grade history class. Her name was Alice and we became instant friends. I don't know why this happens when you're fourteen, and it stops happening by the time you're an adult, it just does. Like when you're young, you accept without question that a snake can propel itself along without appendages, and by the time you hit forty, the snake seems impossible. The older we get, the less willing we are to accept possibility, like a limbless creature making headway, or that of effortless friendship.

"Hey, is he old?" she said, leaning over to my desk.

"Yeah," I said in an eager whisper, trying to discourage her impudence while hoping she'd talk to me again. She didn't.

I thought high school would be different, less exhausting without trying to keep up with Jules, and without Ted of course. I didn't want to be in trouble all the time and I wanted to be friends with the girl in the Levi's.

The high school was built into a hillside. The upper portion galleried the administrative offices and was shaded by eucalyptus columns. Down a pair of switchback ramps was a large concrete atrium lined with lockers and classrooms on one side, and the cafeteria on the other. Another pair of ramps led to the lower parking lot, the locker rooms and the oval track. There was a smoking area, ironically established at the edge of one of the athletic fields.

After class, my history neighbor took off to the atrium, and I saw her meet up with a tall Samoan girl I'd heard sold weed. I headed to my locker, missing Katie, and wondering what high school was like for her and Jules. My locker was next to that of a sweet sandy-haired surfer boy.

★★★

Alice insisted her name was pronounced "Ah-Lee-Cee-Uh" but had given up trying to get people to call her that. She was dazzled by the butterfly I'd drawn on my kraft paper history book cover, and by my willingness to hear her diatribe when the teacher wasn't looking. She talked a lot about guys she hung out with, her cousin—and it was clear that she too was displaced from an established group of friends. That fall, she and I traveled in duplicate and made more friends with the same ease with which she and I had become fellows. Older boys—boys with cars—attended us.

A tall upperclassman named Guy met us at the door the night of the homecoming dance. I'd forgotten my student ID and couldn't get in without it. Guy drove us back to my house to retrieve my credentials. It was my first foray as Alice's wing-girl. This was also the first time my uncle had met my best friend of all of five weeks. I ran to my room and she and Guy waited in the living room. Once I'd located my card among the bed-strewn contents of my book bag, Lawrence came in and loud-whispered to share a little secret with me. He cupped his hand over his mouth and said, "Your friend is wearing evening make-up with jeans."

Once inside the dance, I stood against the wall and stared at the delicious surfer boy whose locker was right next to mine trying to mind-fuck his trinket of a date. I watched them, wondering how she could be so calm, and wishing I had straight hair and slim hips like hers. I never learned his name. I asked him to a dance a few months later and he turned me down. I promptly moved to another locker across the quad.

Alice and Guy stayed at the dance barely an hour before disappearing, presumably in his car. They had a good excuse; Alice lived twenty miles to the south and would have needed a ride home. She was well out of the school district, but her mom—an area police officer—fabricated some paperwork to get Alice into our school. It seems justifiable that, being a cop, Alice's mom would use some inside information to choose a "good" high school for her daughter, most likely employing the district's socio-economic data and juvenile crime stats as her measures for how much trouble her daughter could stay out of.

Later, Alice's mom would ask me a revealing question. I'd phoned one day to find my friend not at home. In fact, her mom didn't know where she was and was worried, citing her teen daughter's recent cryptic behavior.

"Do you know something I don't know?! Is my daughter on drugs?!" She asked.

My reply was non-committal, "I don't know, I don't think so..." and I reveled in the fact that this uber-authority had no idea that her daughter smoked pot, nor that many others in our widening circle did blow or even brought the occasional wine cooler to school. It's unclear whether Alice had been an at-risk-youth before the ninth grade, prompting her mom's school-district subterfuge, or if Alice rebelled in high school despite those efforts to install her among what must have seemed a statistically "safe" student body of upper-middle class teens who were likely just better at hiding their neuroses, crimes, and chemical dalliances.

✦✦✦

Alice's fling with Guy was followed by an attachment to a boy named Jamie. Jamie and Alice looked more like brother and sister than a couple. By Christmas they'd started dressing alike, even sharing clothes. One or the other of them would show up to school in a worn out Iron Maiden t-shirt that I believe was Jamie's, or a too-big (for either of them) grey and yellow flannel shirt that turned out to have belonged to Alice's cousin, or something. The three of us hung out on campus during the day, and walked down the hill to the mall after school. We'd often find a bigger group at the pizza place drinking fountain soda and taking up an entire back corner of the restaurant. Occasionally someone would even have enough money for a tiny cheese pizza or some other cheap snack that they would never share, nor would anyone dare ask.

A junior named Danny brought a bottle of off-brand whiskey one spring afternoon. He had skipped classes that day, and was trying to hock the fifth he'd pilfered from his parents' cabinet when we arrived.

"Hey," I took the empty spot next to him on the end of the bench, plopping my purse—cut from an old quilt and festooned with bandannas—between us and nodded at his pack of smokes. "Can I bum one of those?"

He looked at me, sizing me up: Who was I? What grade was I in? How big were my books? Who were my parents? before affirming, "Sure." He lit my cigarette and said, "I know you."

"Really?" I said, half flattered and half incredulous. Why would a tall, handsome eleventh-grader with broad swimmer's shoulders "know" a freshman with a bad haircut living with mis-matched uncles in a bungalow behind a stable?

He was flirting with my D-cups. "I'm Danny."

"I know." I said. The other guy at the table was leaning toward a girl at the adjacent table, laughing and ignoring us.

"How do you know?"

"Alice said she got high with you before history class." This divulgence of context was beside the fact that everybody knew who he was. Was he blissfully unaware of his own reputation?

He smiled wide and said, "See! You're Alice's friend. I told you I knew you."

An unkempt man I'd never seen before approached, handing Danny the sealed bottle of hooch saying "No go."

"Fuck!" He gripped the glass neck and filled me in. "I'm trying to sell this so I can score some blow." Nestling the bottle on the fabric of my purse, concealing it between us he said, "I guess stank-ass here doesn't have the salesman attitude."

His friend flipped him the bird and walked away, ignoring me in total.

Danny scanned the restaurant, then beyond the glass windows, hoping to spot a pigeon out in the mall. I looked around and caught sight of Jamie and Alice, Jamie straddling the picnic-style bench at a nearby table, Alice sitting in close between his legs, his hand on her ass, his chin on her shoulder as she listened to the others macking at the table. I knew neither of them had any money, and I wasn't even sure either of them had any use for a bottle of whiskey. As teenage girls do, I'd confused Danny's attention for on-the-level affinity, and I'd decided that I wanted to please him.

"I bet I can sell it," I chirped, turning on the charm trying to match his. "What do I do?"

He nodded toward the mall's hallway and said, "Go out there and find some guy who looks like a drinker and ask him if he wants to buy a fifth of whiskey."

"Okay." I said as I grabbed the bottle.

Danny gripped my wrist as I stood, "Leave it here." His touch startled me. "Twenty bucks."

"Okay."

Outside the darkness of the pizza place, shoppers wandered under the skylights. I found a stout guy who smelled like gasoline and I nervously asked him if he wanted to buy a bottle of Jack Daniels for twenty bucks. He stopped, looking kind of dumb, and told my tits, "Sure."

A silent moment passed and he asked, "Where is it?"

"Oh," I said, "my friend has it. He's in there."

Gas-Man pursed his lips in semi-disgust as I ushered him in past Jamie and Alice to Danny's table. We sat and the two men nodded to each other. "Hey man."

"Hey."

Danny produced the bottle, keeping it between their hunched figures. I was quite proud I'd brokered this deal.

"Your dumb blonde here said it was Jack," Gas-Man sputtered when he saw the label.

"You want it or not?" Danny was still charming.

"I'll give you fifteen." Gas-Man looked like a constipated Alfred E. Neuman.

"Nawp. Sorry man, gotta get twenty." Danny shifted his eyes toward the front counter of the pizzeria and I panicked. I felt like a dumbass once again. I was sure we were going to get kicked out and Danny would have wasted his time on a guy that wouldn't even buy the bottle.

Gas-Man sat up straight and looked Danny in the eye. Danny sat up even taller and slid the bottle back in between us. I nervously watched the Round Table cashier. He didn't seem to be paying attention to us.

"All right. What the fuck?" He dug out his wallet and slid two tens toward Danny. "Learn your shit, honey." He reprimanded me, stashing the bottle under his flannel and departing.

I felt so stupid, and didn't know what to say to Danny. I couldn't look at him. My cheeks were hot, and I knew that all that stuff that had gone so well between us for the first twenty minutes was ruined. He probably thought I was the biggest twit in California.

"Fucking good work, partner!" He shoulder checked me, pocketing the cash, flipping his longish blonde hair and lighting a cigarette. The other guy at the table, who was only "at the table" insomuch as he was sitting on the opposite bench with his back to us, leaning into the crowd of girls at the other table, gave us a brief glance, nothing more.

"What did you say your name was, again?" Danny asked.

I was astonished, and thrilled that he was so thrilled. "Connie." I looked at him blinking.

"Yeah... Connie," he said through a Cheshire grin. "I knew that."

✷✷✷

On a Saturday afternoon Alice and I took the bus to hook up with her friend Sheryl. I unnecessarily lied to Lawrence when he asked me where I was going. I told him I was going to the mall to shop with Alice while we waited for Jamie to get done with his music lesson. There was no reason for subterfuge, unless you count the misplaced guilt associated with the fact that the point of the visit was for Alice to buy pot.

Sheryl lived in what I considered to be a nice apartment complex with her father, an airport worker. She was on the front stairs smoking a cigarette when we walked up. I knew her from algebra class, though I'd never talked to her. She had very long, shiny, jet-black ringlets—the front and sides of which were fastened by a silver barrette at the crown. She was wearing a bikini top and gave Alice a hug.

"My dad's sleeping but we can go in my room and get stoned. We just have to be quiet." She put out her cigarette and ushered us up to her second floor apartment.

Hey, you guys wanna go swimming?" She lit a joint and cracked open the slider, the smell of eucalyptus and chlorine swirling in.

"I didn't bring a suit." I said.

She passed the joint to Alice perched on the bed and crossed to a big dresser with an even bigger mirror. "I have extras."

While Sheryl and I probably had the same bust size, she had a smaller frame in general. I couldn't see how a bikini bottom of hers would fit me. That, and the fact that I wouldn't be able to get away with turning down a toke for much longer in this new circle of friends made me nervous. Jamie and Alice had already started giving me a hard time when I didn't smoke out with them.

"Here's one for you." She tossed some orange and green lycra at Alice, who held it up. It was a pretty tropical pattern of hibiscus. "Yeah, that'll work." Alice confirmed, holding the joint out to me. "Here, take this." She peeled off her t-shirt and bra in one motion and fitted the bikini top around her. "It's perfect!" she said, tying the strings and checking the mirror. It was the first time I'd noticed how tan she was.

"You might as well hit that," Alice was referring to the joint. "or give it back to Sheryl."

I was off the hook, and it was a relief. I turned to Sheryl as Alice unbuttoned her jeans.

"Will this work?" Sheryl held up a black and pink bandeau. "You can wear it with your shorts, they don't care."

"Yeah, thanks."

"You done with that?" She pinched the joint and hit it. "You don't smoke?" she asked, holding the hit.

"No, she's our goody-two-shoes!" Alice snorted and they both laughed.

Sheryl stuffed clothes back into the dresser singing "Goody-two, goody-two, goody goody two shoes!" Alice joined in and they mimicked Adam Ant. I couldn't help but laugh.

Sheryl shushed us through a wide grin, reminding us that her dad was sleeping. We put our hands to our mouths and listened a moment before giggling through our noses.

Poolside was awesome. We were the only ones there. Sheryl told us that her dad worked the graveyard shift... and that he was a really cool guy. He let her date a junior with a car even though she was only a freshman. She said her boyfriend would probably stop by. They'd just gotten back together after being broken up for almost five months. They'd split right before New Years, after he'd gotten a hand-me-down car.

"Does *Dan-yel* get along with your dad?" Alice asked, adjusting the towel on her lounge chair. She enunciated 'Daniel' to sound upper-class.

"Yeah." She shrugged and lit a cigarette. "My dad trusts him."

Alice settled back and turned her head toward Sheryl, pulling her sunglasses down over her eyes. "D'you know my cousin?"

Sheryl looked at her thoughtfully for a moment. "Oh! You mean Rich, right?" Her countenance opened up. "Yeah, he was at Danny's last week. They were working on his motorcycle."

I left my uncomfortable lounge chair for the steps in the pool's shallow end. I dipped in and listened to them talk about Sheryl's boyfriend's wealthy parents and their house in the hills. Apparently, a group of guys liked to hang out in the three-car garage tinkering and drinking when the folks weren't home.

I stood in the five-foot depth and leaned on the concrete edge.

"His parents are probably home, otherwise I'd say we should go over there and drink some beer." Sheryl suggested.

I wasn't sure about heading to Danny's or anywhere else, I'd have to get back on the bus soon. Uncle Lawrence would flip out if I was gone all day. But for Danny's parents' presence, I would have had to make some excuse, though drinking beer with a group of guys sounded rather like something I wanted to do.

"There he is." Sheryl stood astraddle the lounge, shaded her eyes and waved at a huge, silver car settling into the parking lot.

Danny strutted up to the iron fence surrounding the pool area and saluted us. "Hey, ladies." Sheryl flip-flopped over for a kiss. It was my booze-hocking partner from the pizza place. I never would have guessed that day that he had a girlfriend. I wasn't disappointed, but I was now interested in him in a non-crush way.

He took a chair under an umbrella and stubbed out a cigarette. He was wearing a t-shirt screen printed with a Ferrari and a helicopter among some palm trees and the phrase "Magnum, p.i." in thick, blocky type.

He and Alice acknowledged each other, and I stayed quiet. I felt like the odd-girl-out again.

"Your cousin's motorcycle is pretty nice," he remarked to Alice.

"He's been saving up for it forever." She was looking at her fingernails, her glasses back on top of her head. "He loves that thing."

"What's he gonna to do with it when he goes into the Army?" Danny sounded like he was fishing.

"I dunno, his dad'll probably hang on to it." She looked up at him, perhaps to read his reaction. "Or maaaaaybe he'll sell it," she said through a grin.

Danny grinned too; Alice leaned back and pushed her face to the sunshine.

Sheryl looked at me, "Connie, this is my boyfriend, Danny."

"Hi," I said.

"Hey." He gave no hint of our acquaintance, and I kept it to myself for the moment.

They discussed Sunday dinner plans and I waded to the center. Dunking myself out of their conversation, I thought about our illicit enterprise, and I wondered if she knew or even cared about the cocaine. Maybe he'd bought it for her. I also wondered why they'd broken up for five months. I wondered if Danny's parents had ever noticed the missing bottle. I flopped around in the water, somersaulting under the surface, coming up for air and looking at the landscaping—whatever I could do to ignore them. I thought about Jamie. I resented Alice for seeming like she didn't miss him. I thought she was a neglectful girlfriend for enjoying the day and displaying zero guilt for having gotten high with Danny, no matter that it was a week ago and one hundred percent her prerogative with whom she got high before history class. A voice in my head said with a wag of the finger that it was improper behavior for a girl—a male voice. But a female voice chalked it up to simply too many secrets—that it was easier and the right thing to do to just be honest. She splashed into the pool next to me, hanging on to her bottoms.

She surfaced near me and pushed her wet hair back. "Whoa! That shit feels good!" Her nose and chin were pinking up.

"What time do you have to meet Jamie?" I asked.

"I don't have to meet him. Besides, Danny just said we should go to his house. His parents are at the beach." She said with a raise of her eyebrows.

"Let's go to my house, I can bring you all back here in a while." He shouted.

Alice whipped around to look at him, then whipped back to me with a huge smile. "Let's do it. Come on, it'll be fun!"

"I'm supposed to be shopping, my uncle thinks I'm going to be back by three."

Danny shouted, "Call him from my house."

Danny's solution had me convinced. "Okay."

We met Danny at his car after changing and climbed into its plush interior. It was a late seventies two-tone silver behemoth. "I'll have to tell my uncle we're at Jamie's or something."

"What if Jamie calls your house?" Alice asked in earnest.

"Oh yeah." I frowned.

"What were you going to tell him about how your hair got wet?" Sheryl asked from the front seat.

I'd forgotten about my hair. It was drying curly and I had no way to straighten it. As Danny drove, I realized I couldn't go.

"You'll have to drop me off at the end of my street," I said.

"Really? Why?" Sheryl asked, turning in her seat to look at me.

"I gotta go home. I'll walk home from there."

Alice said, "Your house is right by there."

Danny looked at me in the rearview, "I can drive you home."

"No way, my uncle will flip out. It's cool, it's only few blocks."

"Okay, but next time..." Danny smiled.

"Definitely."

I climbed out and Alice asked me to tell Jamie she'd call him later. I watched them drive off and wondered why I hadn't the same freedom they all seemed to have. I wondered as I walked home if it originated somehow with Ted, but what was the link? I was at fault for... *what* exactly? What had I done wrong that I couldn't build trust? What was I being penalized for?

Lawrence tapped on my open door while I sat on my bed writing a letter to Katie.

"What'd you find at the mall?" he asked. "Anything good?"

"No, we just had some fries and watched the ice skaters," I lied.

He sat down on the edge of my hope chest and said, "So…"

I looked up at him.

He continued. "You know this isn't an ideal situation… for either of us. But Ted's got to go live his life now, and your mom's off doing gawd knows what."

We'd been there three months, and I'd thought it was going okay—not great, but at least okay. I listened with caution.

"And your grandmother already put in her time raising kids, she's done with all that, she can't do it again," he said. "I'm all you got, kid,"

I was relieved he wasn't sending me somewhere else, but his curt speech contained a disappointing subtext. All I could say was, "I know."

"Okay, I'm glad we got to talk," he said, "so we understand each other."

He got up and stepped out of the room, then turned at the door and added, "Next time you're at the mall, you should buy some clothes. Those jeans aren't doing you any favors. Girls like you shouldn't wear pegged pants."

"Well, since I don't have any money, I guess I'm going to have to wear these."

He looked at me for a moment, then said, "We'll get Gram to buy you some clothes."

He left the room and I sat on my bed feeling worn out. I looked out the window at the small guest cottage in the back. Will was at work. I felt alone again, and I didn't know what to write to Katie.

✦✦✦

Jamie and I sat in patio chairs in my uncle's back yard and bullshitted about the guy from whom he'd bought the joint he was about to smoke. Thoroughbreds snorted behind us.

"I think Cliff," he said, digging for his lighter, "is a retard." He scrunched his nose as he said 'retard,' and talked in a small boy's voice. He did this to illustrate some irony. It was Jamie's thing, his charm. He had a hawk nose on a freckled, green-eyed boy face. Cliff was a goofy guy, and dense, but reasonably in control of his faculties otherwise.

"I love this song." I said.

"Billy Idol sucks," he said.

"Well, aren't you Mr. Happy today," I said.

His demeanor improved and he looked at me and said, "Hey, my mom's buying me a guitar."

"Oh yeah! Your birthday is right after the fourth of July..." I said.

Jamie finished Cliff's pinner joint and lit a cigarette. "Yup." He held the pack of smokes out to me and I pulled one, but didn't light it. "My mom wants you to come over for dinner on my birthday," he said.

"Really?"

"Well yeah. You're my best friend, right?" He shrugged and tugged at the front of his Motley Crüe t-shirt with his thumb and ring finger.

"What about Alice?" I asked, looking down at my foot, pulling a blade of grass with my toes.

"She didn't sound especially excited when I told her about it." He looked befuddled. "Kinda like she has other plans that day."

"Doesn't she hang out at her cousin's on Saturday nights?" I asked.

"Well, yeah, but why is that more important than my birthday?"

"I dunno."

I wondered if she was trying to break up with him. They'd been together practically the whole school year. I wondered if there was another guy in the group that hung out at her cousin's. She'd gone to junior high with those people before her mom sent her to our school. I didn't want to say it to Jamie, but I thought she was losing interest in him, though she wouldn't tell me if she was.

"What?" he said, eyeballing me.

I replayed his question, though I had no idea to what it pertained. "What?" I asked back.

"You went all quiet," he said, scrunching his nose again.

"What. I was just trying to figure out what was so important at her cousin's house."

"I think she's doing coke," he said off-handedly. "Hey, by the way, did I tell you? Cliff's brother is a free-baser!" This bit of gossip earned enthusiasm, and once again I was stuck either asking the dumb question, or just nodding and pretending to know what free-basing was.

"What the hell is free-basing? That guy I was telling you about, Judd, he mentioned it."

"It's smoking coke."

"Oh... Really? How do you smoke coke? I've heard of people sprinkling some in a cigarette. Is it like that?"

"No, it's different. I'm not really sure how they do it." He thought a moment. "I think it has to be pure, or something."

"Huh. I've never done coke." I said.

Chapter Four: Or The Highway

Jamie and Alice broke up unofficially before Halloween. Alice spent more and more time with her friends in Redwood City, less time with us, and was unapologetic about it. A rumor surfaced that she was sleeping with her cousin. Jamie's response was to spend a few intense weeks with a homeless girl named Christy, and I was sure it was Christy who'd started the rumor. Jamie's charitable mom let Christy spend nights in Jamie's bedroom, though he claimed he never touched her, even as she lounged on his bedroom floor listening to records in nothing more than one of his t-shirts, undies, and socks. I had no reason not to believe him.

I called him every day for almost a week when I finally caught him at home. "I want you to meet my friend Judd. He's going to be in town for the weekend!"

"The guy from the valley?" Jamie asked.

"Yeah, you'll like him. He smokes weed." I was ecstatic. We made plans to hang out all day Saturday.

"So… are you guys serious now?"

"I don't know, and I don't care!"

Judd would be taking a bus in on Friday, he'd told me his truck needed some work. We'd talked a lot that summer following a spring break tryst. I'd gone back to visit Katie. A boy in her neighborhood had a hot tub and his parents were away on vacation. We invited Judd and he supplied the beer. By the end of the night, he and I were alone. We hadn't been considering ourselves a long-distance couple, but there was something there. I'd tried a couple times to talk him into coming, and I was thrilled he was finally making the trip.

Jamie and I met Judd outside the hotel he'd spent the night in. He checked out, and our plan was to find him lodging for the coming night, and to hook up with our friend Rob. I felt like a queen. Judd and Jamie were my two favorite men in the world. We rode the bus to the apartment Rob shared with his mom.

We knocked on Rob's door and could hear "Shout at the Devil" playing inside.

"Hey! Come on in!" Rob was in a good mood, and his mom was at work. "What's up guys?" He turned the stereo down a little. Jamie made introductions and the two guys nodded in acknowledgment. Rob was animate, and Judd clocked him.

"Dude, where's that girl you've been hangin' with?" Rob asked after Christy.

"She's in juvie." Jamie's answer was a surprise to me as I'd been so preoccupied with Judd I'd forgotten to ask.

"What happened?" I said.

Jamie was nonchalant. "Oh nothing, she was a runaway. They'll send her back to Nevada." Jamie crinkled his nose and admitted in a low voice, "She was only thirteen." He and Rob low-fived and Judd stood stoic.

"Hey Rob, do you have some weed." I asked.

"Do I have some weed? Girl, who do you think you're talking to?" He plopped down on the couch in front of the biggest homemade bong I've ever seen, and we found seats around him. Judd sat in an armchair and insisted I sit on his lap. I was relieved he wasn't mad at me. The guys smoked and I snuggled against Judd, breathing in second-hand marijuana smoke. Jamie lit a cigarette and I bummed a couple drags of it.

"That's bad for you." Judd's comment was sharp and cold. "Get up," he ordered.

I'd done something wrong. I stood up almost not quick enough as he rose, his face in mine and said, "Can I talk to you?"

"Okay—"

"In there." He pointed to the kitchen.

The countertop was littered with wine cooler bottles and cut-open cans emptied of their pork 'n' beans or spaghetti-rings.

"I have something for you, do you want it or not?"

I didn't know what I'd done to piss him off. "What's wrong?" He didn't answer me, so I countered with my hands on my hips. "Maybe I don't want your present!"

He stepped back gripping the edge of the sink with one hand and waved the other at me balled in a fist. "Sometimes I just wanna slam you against the nearest wall and make you listen!" He threw up both hands in disgust, lunging toward me and gasped, "Uuhhh!"

"Whad'you get me?" I asked right as Rob increased the volume on the stereo,

Judd moved in on me, backing me up against the far kitchen wall and asked, with a tilt of his head, "Excuse me?"

I was afraid, but more afraid to back down. I shouted, "I want the present," and held out my hand.

He shook his head and exited the drab kitchen pulling me by my wrist.

Back in the living room Judd announced, "Hey man, I'm gonna need a place to crash tonight," and settled his arm around my neck, turning on the charm. The guys came to attention and Rob reached over to turn the stereo down.

"Man, if my mom stays out late, you can seriously crash here." Rob bopped into the kitchen and I looked at Jamie, who was sunken into a papasan chair examining the hem of his shirt.

Judd reclaimed his armchair throne and eyed me. I

sat on the couch near Jamie and asked, "What's up?"

"Nothing, I'm fuckin' high." Jamie rolled his eyes up to Judd. I didn't feel like humoring his moodiness. It was clear he didn't like Judd, and I just wanted them to get along.

"Dammit! No more wine coolers." Rob emerged from the kitchen and asked what time it was. "If my mom doesn't come home right after work, it means she's with her boyfriend, and might not come home." Rob was triangulating, holding his hands palm-to-palm, fingertips-to-fingertips in front of his chin, then shot them both out pointing at us. "Let's go cruise around for a while."

The four of us wandered the avenue and ended up at my house to find Lawrence gone, and Will in the cottage. Will got stoned with the guys, initiating fervent discourse about issues topical to teenage men. Will and Rob engaged in a lively conversation, while Jamie and Judd and I sat in semi-silence, the two of them occasionally eyeing each other.

Rob asked to use the phone, keen to find out if he and Judd would have an uninterrupted party night at his mom's apartment. Judd's ability to buy alcohol served as a solid lodging fee for the night.

Rob hung up the phone and smiled big. "What it is, my man!" He happily reported, "My sweet mama, wherever she is, should be nice and drunk!"

"She's not home, huh?" Judd asked through heavily-reddened eyes.

"Nope. And even if she does come home, she'll be too drunk to care. Shall we?"

"I'll walk up to the bus with you guys." I preferred to elude Lawrence, even though he knew Judd was in town. I couldn't think of a reason for them to meet. He usually had nice things to say about my female friends, and he went for the low-hanging fruit when it came to pointing out my male friends' flaws. Lawrence could be counted on to spotlight the hallmarks of growing up poor: a bad haircut, hand-me-down clothes, an unmet need for braces, or generally being common. He never missed a chance at a slight, although somehow Jamie was always spared a ride on his derision train.

We spilled out of the guest house and onto the back patio, Jamie and Will discussing the cut and fit of Jamie's corduroys. Uncle Will always had nice things to say about my guy friends. The girls were mostly invisible to him, even the pretty ones. But not the boys.

We didn't make our exit quite fast enough. Lawrence appeared at the glass slider. He smiled and waved to us, and I introduced him to Judd. Jamie and Rob greeted him and headed around for the gate, Will in tow.

"This is Judd," I said. "He's going back to Sac in the morning."

"Hello Judd, how's life in Sacra-tomato?" Lawrence

stood two concrete steps above us in the door frame.

"Oh it's a bowl of cherries," Judd said with a coolness that stopped just short of hostility.

"Connie's mother calls it the armpit of California." He was brilliant at lobbing an insult and deflecting responsibility for it. But any disdain Judd might have felt had nothing to do with an offhand denigration of his hometown. He simply didn't defer to adults, especially father-figures.

"Are you staying with Will tonight?" The question startled me, I'd never thought to ask, and I answered before Judd could.

"No, I'm going to walk them up to the bus." I wanted to get out of there. "We have to go, I'll be right back." Judd extended a handshake to Lawrence as Will hurried by in his stocking feet, padding up the guest house path waving a goodbye-and-nice-to-meet you to Judd.

The four of us hoofed it up to the bus stop. Judd and I lagged behind and eventually stopped. He handed me his duffel and bade me hold it up. He rifled through it and produced a folded piece of paper.

"Thank you," he said as he re-zipped it and grabbed its handles. The piece of paper was my present.

It was a pencil sketch of a knight on a horse with a broadsword and a banner that read "Death Before Dishonor." He'd drawn it, he said. His artistic ability overshadowed his earlier belligerence.

I called him at Rob's that night. Jamie had already gone home and Rob was playing Atari. We talked for over an hour until Lawrence tugged on the phone cord stretched under my bedroom door.

✦✦✦

Sheryl and I made a pilgrimage on a Sunday afternoon in the spring to a park in my new neighborhood. Lawrence had sold the stable-side bungalow and the three of us moved into a bigger house a few blocks from school. I'd started working part time at the mall, but my boss usually didn't schedule me on the weekends, which was fine with me. I much preferred to work nights after school. Sheryl and I journeyed there to examine the site where a girl from the next town over had been attacked, and to hang out, and maybe get some burgers for lunch.

We were near a grouping of benches, standing there with our big purses, looking at the ground. I imagined moonlight and shadows outlining heavy boot prints in the mud, and a girl our age lying alone after midnight, still and prone, blood pooling in the hollows of her shut eyes. Her name was Lisa, a very common name, but she also shared a less common last name with a friend of mine who'd moved to the same town the previous summer.

"Fuckin' —A…" was all we could say, while Lisa

recovered in a bed at the medical center a mile or so away.

"She was the one at your birthday party?" Sheryl puzzled.

"No no, it's not her. I forgot to tell you." We'd heard most of the details of the attack from people at school, rumors swirling in the quad and exaggerations in the locker room over the previous week. Finally and thankfully, a school photo of the girl published in the paper revealed that it was not my relocated friend.

"Ohhh, okay." Sheryl said, with a look that acknowledged it didn't matter which one of us it was or wasn't. "But still..."

"Yeah, no shit." I answered.

When we tired of staring at cut grass and acorns, we plopped down at a stone bench to smoke. We talked about those who were alive and uninjured: Danny, Jamie, our math teacher, Sting. We talked about walking to over for some chicken tenders. I hadn't left my uncle a note and would need to get home by four or so. He'd gone to church and was planning to drive to Gram's for the afternoon. A scruffy dude at another bench had been hunched over scratching something into the seat of it, but had now taken an interest in us. I glanced at him every so often, and this time he was erect and staring us down.

"Do you know that guy?" Sheryl asked.

"No. But he's coming over here." The man rose and executed a series of twists with his left wrist, afterward jamming the hand into his trouser pocket. He'd closed and concealed a butterfly knife. I only knew that's what it was because Jamie had one with perforated brass handles. He'd taught me how to flip it open and closed.

The man stood in front of us. He was wearing too many shirts.

"Hey, I'm not a weirdo or anything." He wasn't much older than we were. "I just wanted to say 'hi' and see if I could bum a dime."

"I've got some change," Sheryl said and pulled a slitted rubber coin pouch from her bag.

The man plopped down in the grass in front of us and reached into the pocket of his oversized flannel outershirt.

"Oh." He made a little noise and looked down at his pocket, tugging at the front tail of the shirt to keep it taut.

"Ohhhh my gaaaawwwwddd!" Sheryl cooed, her eyes widening.

"Is it alive?" I asked when I saw what he was holding.

The grey and white fur quaked in his cupped hands and Sheryl leaned in to get a better look at what seemed to be the cutest kitten in California.

"He's the runt. He can open his eyes, he's just been sleeping."

Sheryl insisted on holding him, and the babe stretched in her palms, pushing two tiny white paws in the air and opening its mouth.

"He's older than he looks." The man assured us that he was old enough to be off mother's milk, but he still needed some food.

"Don't you need to get him home for feeding?" I said.

"We're homeless. That's why I was hoping you guys had some spare change."

"Oh yeah, no problem." Sheryl said. "This little guy is going to need to be fed four times a day... at least." She handed the squirmy kitten to me and emptied her coin purse into the man's hands.

"Oh thank you!" He stood up so fast it startled us both. "Hey, can you guys watch him for a minute? I need to go get some supplies."

"Sure," we said, and Sheryl mentioned a store around the corner.

"Great." He turned and stopped. "Actually, I have to go to a friend's house to pick up a fanny pack. My buddy is fixing it so the cat can ride in it."

"Oh, okay." Sheryl and I looked at each other. "Should we come with you?"

"Naw, it's just right by here." He turned forty-five degrees and walked off saying, "I'll be back." I rubbed the kitten on my cheek, and we smiled at each other.

When I looked back up at the man, he was striding a beeline to the West, then turned, in the middle of the park, another forty-five degrees and continued along the new trajectory.

The kitty kept us occupied for a while. We let him walk around on the concrete tabletop, dragged the corner of her bandanna in front of him as a makeshift toy, and giggled at his clumsiness. He was a runt, but certainly not sickly, and he did open his eyes.

"What time is it?" I asked and scanned the park. There was no one else there aside from an ownerless dog carrying out a sniff inventory of every tree.

Sheryl consulted her ring watch. "It's almost four. He's been gone over an hour."

"I'm hungry." I suggested we get lunch, keeping our tiny companion concealed in one of our purses, and hope we run into the man on the way back. We could get a milkshake for the kitten.

"Don't you have to be home by four?"

"I can't go home with a kitten, my uncle wouldn't be very happy."

"I can't take him, we live in an apartment," she countered.

"I know." We both sighed and scanned the park. The dog was gone.

Our return from lunch was just as fruitless. We sat at the same bench and ate our lunch. By five-thirty, the best plan we could come up with was to walk around the area and look for the man, and that's what we did. The later it got, the more I knew I'd get an earful when I got home, and that it would be much worse if I had a kitten in my purse.

We walked exasperated up the avenue and a big stupid car pulled up beside us. I was grumpy and thought it was some joker flirting, then I realized it was Danny and I felt hopeful. For no valid reason I thought the presence of a guy would make everything better. We crawled into his car and briefed him as we drove around. At six forty-five there was still no sign of Kitten-Man and I instructed Danny to take me home.

Sheryl came in with me to help explain the situation to Uncle Lawrence, which turned out to be pointless. He was acrimonious, but the cat was just an excuse. I went to my room and slammed the door, plopping down frustrated on the edge of the bed and held the sleepy animal.

Sheryl came in and handed me a photocopy. "Your uncle wanted me to give you this." It read:

Tired of Being Harassed By Your Stupid Parents?
Act Now! Move Out... Get a Job... Pay Your Own Bills.
Do it While You Still Know Everything

"Danny's still waiting outside, let's just go," she said.

I looked at her. I knew what she was suggesting, but I couldn't do it. I was scared, and I had nowhere left to go. "I'll walk you out." I conceded.

We stepped into the hallway and she said, "I'd take the kitten if I could."

"It's okay."

Lawrence appeared at the end of the hall and shouted, "I don't want you here anymore!"

We froze in place.

He straightened, sighed, pointed at me, and reiterated, "I don't want you here if that's how you're going to act." He wasn't angry this time.

Sheryl looked back at me, eyes wide. I whispered, "Wait for me," and slunk back into my room.

I grabbed what I could stuff into a bag. Lawrence wasn't violent, but I knew he meant what he'd said. I'd never felt completely welcome, nor deserving living in his home, a hallmark of toxic patriarchy. He wasn't cruel like in the movies, but he'd made it clear that there was no two-way relationship between us. He'd said as much.

At one point he'd enlisted the help of his close friend, an affable priest to counsel me after he and Gram had decided I needed guidance. I did, but a man in a cassock wasn't the answer. I was uncomfortable as he asked me semi-personal questions. I had, at best, short, guarded answers for him, and that was the first and last 'counseling session' we would have. Lawrence was neither financially nor emotionally equipped to nurture someone else's embattled fifteen-year-old daughter. Gram had helped him with the down payment on the house behind the racetrack, but in the end he couldn't make the commitment required; four years and some sympathy for the female perspective, as well as the selflessness required to be a parent. Lawrence's favorite one-liner had, after all, been "My way or the highway." It had been engineered to fail, probably from the moment Ted had branded me ungrateful.

I'd left the kitten in my open purse on the bed and now I couldn't find it. I searched and Sheryl stood just outside the door like a sentinel. I found the animal under the bed, settled him into my bag, and left yet another room of mine that turned out to be temporary.

Even with Sheryl at my side, the walk down the hallway to the open of the living room was like being in a thriller and not knowing the position of the intruder. He wasn't in sight, but the front door was. I thought it took a week to reach it, but off we went.

Danny saw us coming and inquired when we got in the car, "No shit, a sleepover on a school night?"

"Her uncle kicked her out," Sheryl said.

"Whaaaat? Over a cat?" He turned to look at me over the seat. "Where are you going to go?"

"Doesn't your mom live in the city?" Sheryl asked.

"Yeah, but she has her own life," I said. I slumped in the seat and checked on the kitten in my bag. I'd snuggled him into a wadded up flannel shirt and he was sound asleep. "I have an auntie, but she hates me. None of my family will let me stay with them."

"You know what, my dad will let you stay for one night." She thought a moment. "I'll tell him you and your uncle got in a fight. I'll tell him your uncle is just being an asshole or something. I think he'll be cool."

"Okay."

"Oh, but we can't tell him about the kitten."

"Okay."

✦✦✦

We took the bus to school in the morning, and I hauled my gear and the kitten in my purse to five of my six classes. I ditched last period to find the kitten's owner. I had to work that evening in the food court.

I detoured through the park on my way to the mall. The son of a bitch wasn't there.

I'm always fascinated by people who are adamant about not having kids, gawd bless 'em and their commitment to themselves. It's a schtick for them. I don't mean people who aren't ready, I mean those who regard kids almost as contemptible aliens. Myself, I've always had this sort of Freudian slip regarding children versus adults of referring to the adults as 'humans,' like when you talk about the two tables at Thanksgiving dinner. I have to correct myself that it's 'kids and adults,' not 'kids and humans.' It's a little glitch in my lingual matrix. It's always been there.

I figured Lawrence was right when he'd declared he was my last chance. There was no point in calling Gram, and certainly not Elyse. I was sure they all shared Lawrence's sentiment. I didn't belong among them.

"Hey."

I didn't know what I was going to do after work. My shift was over at nine. When I thought about it, I pictured myself squatting in the shrubbery outside Jamie's window. But I couldn't pictu—

"HEY!"

I stopped and looked. Kitten-Man was standing on the front porch of a large, shabby house, one sneakered foot stuck under a plastic bag of trash. He jumped down the steps and met me on the sidewalk. "C'mon, let's go to the park," he said.

I was so happy to see him and I told him the heartfelt if not literal story that we'd been looking everywhere for him all this time.

"Uh hunh." He was listening to me as we walked and I unzipped my purse to show him the fat, sleepy animal.

"Do you know my name?" he asked.

I stopped, wondering why he would ask that. "No—"

"Why'd you try to steal my cat?" He was walking in front of me, and this time he wore only one shirt, a dirty Le Tigre polo. His arms were badly scratched and scarred.

"We didn't."

He turned to look at me, walking backwards. The park was only a block further. "Where's your friend?"

Again, I didn't get his motivations and all I could do was blink at him. "She's at school."

"It's shitty to steal someone's pet. Y'know that?"

"We didn't steal him. Here, take him." I stopped and held my bag open and he extracted the creature.

"We're going to go sit in the park for a while. You should apologize." He was cross, and his eyes were cold and narrow.

"Girls like you…"

"I have to go." I took a test step. He had no more accusations for me.

He watched me take another step and turn. I hurried off. I felt him there but didn't look back.

✸✸✸

I crashed on my boss' living room floor that night, and for the rest of the week. I would have slept on the couch but she didn't have one. I called Jamie and he reassured me that my uncle would take me back. He didn't get it. And I couldn't ask Jamie to ask him mom if I could stay there. I'd seen how that worked out for Christy. I knew that clinging to Jamie would be temporary, better not to cling at all. By the end of the week I'd exhausted all but my only option; I kept circling back around to Judd.

My boss was sweet, and we'd had fun during the week, but she wanted her living room floor back. She had a three-year-old to care for, and she was about to get married. She was happy to hug me goodbye and wish me well in the parking lot of her apartment complex. Judd had been about two and half hours late picking me up, ironically about how long it takes to drive from the valley to the peninsula. We drove back in Judd's blue truck with his friend Steve riding shotgun. The guys made jokes about Judd driving at night with his sunglasses on and waxed silly about the mind-bending refractions of the highway lights. I didn't know what they were talking about until a few months later when the phenomenon was cited as typical of an LSD trip.

Chapter Five: A Year in a Bucket

I shared a room with Nicole. Her bed had a trundle underneath it, and the room was filled with stuff, girly stuff. The only way to pull out the trundle was to stack most of her toys and boxes against one wall. The eight-year-old watched me move her things around asking questions and directing the project. I'd sleep about ten inches off the floor on a mattress about five inches thick.

Judd was my boyfriend when I moved in, and he would sneak past the girl and wake me, always saying he wanted to show me something, as if the ruse was necessary. I'd always sneak with him. His room was in the back of the house off the dining room, out of range of the rest of the sleeping family. The two dogs were always right outside, usually cozied up against the glass slider, but never made a noise when Judd and I would stay up later than the rest of the household, being alone together.

Judd's mom, Shelly, had a bottomless bucket of anecdotes about family dynamics, the telling of which usually painted her as a classic mother figure and Judd as some unsung hero, Jason as a lost boy, and Nate as the shy one. Nicole was her sassy cherub. Her stories were saccharine, but her very real discipline was like an acid bath. She showered me with attention right off, and I placed my trust in her and Nicole. Shelly was probably happy to have an older girl in the house, and maybe she was on her best behavior for another reason. Judd and Jason were her natural sons, and Nicole and Nate were adopted. As a foster placement I came with a stipend from the state. Shelly's days were bursting with her kids, in one way or another.

Judd's thirteen year-old brother, Jason—a.k.a. Frisbee-Boy—soon became enamored of his older brother's girlfriend and his mother's new favorite ward.

Carl, Shelly's husband, had an oversized wood desk in a disheveled office off the master bedroom. The desktop was home to the usual long-forgotten home office items including an old typewriter. One summer day I asked Shelly if I could use it and she indulged me. I typed for the better part of the afternoon, tapping out nineteen pages of a draft about a pair of platonic teens thumbing it to San Diego straight out of high school. About an hour in Shelly poked her head in and asked if I wanted anything. I didn't. About an hour later, Jason wandered into the office and asked what I was doing. I answered, and he followed up with about a half dozen more inane questions as I became more and more annoyed. He stood quietly next to the desk for a few minutes, a basketball under his arm then slipped out. I continued writing. I could hear Shelly and Jason arguing outside the door every now and then, and I felt, for the first time like I had my own vantage point on this odd family, a sort of duck blind.

Thump... Thump... Thump... Thump...

I could also write. That was the best part.

Thump... Thump... Thump... Thump... Thump...

By the time the thumping started to get on my nerves I realized it had been going on for a while. Jason was in the back yard bouncing his basketball off the wall of the office—the wall that was about three feet from my head. Shelly appeared in the doorway. "Okay, Connie, that's enough," she hissed. "You two are going to drive me crazy. Go on, get out." She directed me out of the office and pulled the door shut tight behind us. I never got to use the typewriter again.

✹✹✹

The high school in the valley offered an auto shop class, a fine drama department, and two back-to-back pottery classes for my creative indulgence during that year. In acting class, I found out what a stage kiss was, and when I didn't get a part in the school's production of a murder mystery, I was asked to work on props in my two hours of ceramics class. I customized and fired a trio of pre-fomed Buddha statuettes to be smashed onstage during the two performances. I painted them each in their own unique and showy color schemes, sparing no hue or flourish. If they were to have a short existence, I meant for it to be a passionate one. I'm not sure what became of the third figurine. I also designed an enormous mushroom with a thick shaft and a pair of smaller, spherical fungi at its base. The top of my erection was a removable bowl. I was allowed to work in the back of the room where the instructor put up a drape presumably to cover his ass more than censor my erotic pottery. There was a strict policy against students making pipes or bongs, but this was neither so I was allowed to shape my phallic vision in clay as other students grinned and tittered. There was no particular reason why I made a mushroom-cock except that I needed to create. The world always came up so damn wrong, but when I was creating, it would all spin just right, for a little while at least. These classes and new friends kept me occupied while the State of California sorted out who would end up with parental custody of me.

Midway through the school year one of Judd's friends hosted a party at the river, issuing hand-drawn, psychedelic fliers during the week leading up to the event. The municipal banks of the American River provided a fantastic venue for high schoolers seeking a late-night trip and whatever misadventures might accompany tabs on tongues. The air was crisp and inviting under the stars and a footbridge over a narrow provided us with our acid-trip playground. We could loiter in the park on one side, at the utility station on the opposite shore, on the bridge above the dark water, or on either bank. Judd and I rode over in his truck and sat in the parking lot for a few minutes. He recognized some of the other cars, and we could just see the figures on the bridge they called the "Little Golden Gate." He handed me a tiny paper square instructing me to put it on my tongue and I did.

We met up with his friends Steve and Matt on the bridge and I stared at the water while they bullshitted, establishing that someone named Laura wasn't there yet. I spat out the tiny wad of paper, and wondered if I was supposed to have swallowed it. I felt more bored than anything. I looked at the river and remembered a rafting trip when I was ten. The Watsons had come for a visit, and the six of us floated the American River in a rental. Mindy ended up with a bad sunburn, and Ted and my mom argued over whether or not I should have to wear a life vest the length of our leisurely float, Ted finally winning out and securing the orange device around me. Mary Watson had worn high-heeled wedges and the men had a tough time not paddling us in circles. I didn't remember what section of the river we'd been on, but I think I would have remembered if we'd passed under a bridge that looked like the Golden Gate. San Francisco was the love of my mom's life.

"I gotta go get some supplies." Judd looked at me. "You stay here?" It was a question and a suggestion, I believe.

"Okay."

Matt handed him some cash and confirmed the beer brand and quantity.

Steve called out before turning to finish crossing the bridge, "And Laura."

"And Laura," Judd answered with a grin. "I'll be back."

"Let's go." Matt motioned us in the opposite direction, toward the locked outbuilding. Steve was a few paces ahead of us and I could see he was smoking something. When we caught up with him, he asked me how I felt.

"I don't feel anything," I said.

"Nothing?" Matt asked. "How many hits did you take?"

"Judd gave me one."

"Well here." He handed me another small paper square from a tiny container in his shirt pocket. He assured me that'd be about right, and the three of us joined another group smoking joints on the backside of the utility station. The grass was tall around the brick structure, and the shrubs were dry and unpleasant to touch. We crossed that bridge repeatedly, from the wild side to the manicured side and back again. The constituency of the group changed each time, as some stayed where the pot was being smoked, and others stayed near the cars in the parking lot. But I kept crossing, following along behind whomever was making the journey across the deck, which seemed to have a more pronounced texture with each pass. On one pass, I thought the surfaces had been switched out. I swore I was walking along the river's surface, while the bridge's asphalt sheeting seemed to be lying below in the riverbed.

A fire on the wild bank caught my eye and I was overcome with guilt as I was afraid I'd started it. I was terrified, and I hurried over. The closer I got, the bigger the flames got and I saw that some people were feeding the blaze with beach wood. I stopped and realized in a flash of staggering genius that I wasn't smoking anything, and couldn't have started the fire.

Aside from breathing, I couldn't think of a single thing we were doing that night that wasn't in violation of some local ordinance, state law, or federal statute. I made my way down to the shore. The underside of the bridge bore typical criss-cross steel supports and was surprisingly accessible back where it met the pier anchor. I didn't know any of the people on the beach quite well enough to talk to. I looked up and saw that someone had climbed into the supports, compelling me to do the same.

Being up under the bridge felt like hanging on the underside of a ship in space. The black steel, the blue of the night, and the gold from the fire made a wicked argyle. The further out I scooted along the beams, the longer became the drop to the sand below, but the river called, and I found myself impressed by my own climbing prowess. I sat on a beam for a while at the farthest spot I felt like climbing out to, dangling my legs above the water's edge. Someone advised from below "Don't fall!" and giggled. I looked back at where I'd crawled from and was bewildered not to find the other monkey. I thought I'd been aware of his presence as I'd been picking my way along, yet I didn't notice him climbing back out, nor dropping to the beach. Being there alone now disagreed with me and I set out to climb back. I wondered if I'd been there longer than the few minutes I thought I had. Maybe an hour had passed. Maybe more. I was worried that Judd was back and couldn't find me, and I had a feeling he'd be pissed. I started to make my way back to a spot that looked like the shortest drop onto soft sand, but as my right hand gripped a beam I realized I wasn't alone after all. In the negative spaces created by the criss-crossing beams, I saw silhouettes of oversized spiders, about one per space. I hadn't noticed them while I was climbing out, and I wondered how the hell I could have missed them. They were the size of bread plates though perfectly still. Not wanting to have to pick my way back through the arachni-minefield, I readied myself to drop from that spot. It was closer to the rocky, sand-compacted water's edge than I would have liked, but it was either that or crawl among spiders that technically shouldn't have even been in North America, let alone in such a large grouping under a bridge in central California. I let go. The fall seemed to take longer than it should, but I landed without incident, retrieved my purse, and sidled up to Matt by the fire.

"Where have you been?" he asked. "Judd couldn't find you."

"Right here," I said.

"We gotta meet 'em at the park," Matt said.

Steve drove Matt, me, and a girl named Danielle to a wooded park across town, and the clock in his car read 10:17. It had been just over two hours since Judd and I had parked at the river. We stopped at a store and Danielle and I waited in the back seat of the Honda while the guys went in. I was trying to tell Danielle who Judd was when I looked out the tiny car window and found him staring me down. He was parked just opposite us.

"Oh fuck!" I giggled. "He's right there!" I jumped out of the car and Danielle followed.

His truck was full of people, including his blonde Native American neighbor, Hope, and he said, "Going to the park, right?"

I looked back at Danielle and said, "Come on," as we climbed into the back of the truck.

Judd angled out of his open window and caught me in his rear view, offering a sincere apology, though

I wasn't sure what for. He idled just long enough to confirm to Steve and Matt that he'd commandeered their females, then the small convoy took to the road.

At the park, under giant oak trees we found a bench, and I was introduced to Laura and Hope, the girls riding with him. We drank and listened to Steve and Laura tell stories about Grateful Dead shows. I couldn't figure the connection; whether they were siblings and had grown up on tour, or if they were conflating other people's stories, or mixing in stories from other concerts. I didn't know where Laura fit in, whose girlfriend she was, what was real and what wasn't. I didn't tell anyone about the spiders. Someone offered me a line of crank and I snorted it without asking what it was.

Steve and Laura went for a walk and Danielle and I went to read the graffiti on a nearby backboard while Hope sat at the bench and loaded a bowl. I saw Judd march off and I moved to the dark side of the backboard and lit a cigarette. A peace symbol carved at eye level into the backstop started to look like a butterfly.

"Yeah, I don't know him," Danielle told me, referring to Judd. "I just transferred."

"He graduated last year," I told her, as I watched the butterfly become a clown's face.

"Where were you last year?" she asked.

"The bay area." The clown was trying to tell me

something.

"Where?" She asked from the other side of the plywood wall. I didn't answer. I was reading the clown's lips, and I thought it was saying, 'More to do,' or 'more than two.' I had the urge to paint the other side of the backstop with a giant clown—a mural so big it could be seen all the way across the park, with a big voice bubble of whatever the hell it was the clown was trying to say to me. 'Fortitude?'

"Hellloooo?" She called after a few minutes of me not answering her.

The clown was gone, and the peace symbol was silent but vibrating. I labored a moment to recall her question, then said, " You know where San Francisco is?"

"Duh..." she said.

"This is about the dumbest conversation I've ever heard," came a male voice.

I jumped and cracked a nervous smile at Judd leaning on the edge of the backboard. He grabbed my right hand and pulled the cigarette from my left one, burning the middle finger on my right hand and tossing the cigarette away in one motion.

"Ow!"

"Ow..." he mocked over my cry. "Smoking is dangerous to your health. Don't you know that, little girl?"

A family camping trip had the three younger kids rummaging through their closets, shouting out of turn, and fighting over anything they could fight over. The six of us would leave Carl over the spring school break and head to the campground. Judd and I rode up in his truck, after I turned down Nicole's plea to ride with us. She and Jason had lied only a week previous—separately, no less—to Shelly about how a lamp had gotten broken, and the fallout had landed squarely on me. The sibling rivalry and gamesmanship were a bit of fun I'd never experienced before, and those two were grandmasters. Nate was the quiet devious one. Shelly had told me that his misbehaviors included things like emptying a syrup bottle into his sleeping sister's hair, or walloping her from behind on the playground for no reason. A few months after I moved in Nate put bleach in the hair conditioner bottle, and Shelly fell for it. I was the blonde in the house, and Shelly blamed an extremely puzzled me. I was unnerved by the success of his caper, and disappointed that she thought I was dumb enough to consider laundry bleach and conditioner a hair-lightening formula.

Judd's miscreant behaviors were more mature and included things like emotionally abusing Nicole, growing pot on the roof of his mother's state approved foster home, and assembling homemade pipe bombs. Nicole acted out in the typical ways: smuggling a bikini to school in her lunch box and stealing my jewelry. Loyalties were constantly shifting, we were like too many cats, but messier.

Shelly had reserved two tipis for the campout. I'd been in the foster home nine months, and Judd and I had long since stopped our late night romantic sneak-arounds. She always caught us, anyway. She'd reserved the extra tipi for us knowing we'd settled into a sibling-esque friendship, even though he'd chased my friend Jimmy with a baseball bat when Jimmy hadn't repaid him quite quickly enough with the proceeds from a loaned sheet of acid. Shelly, always the doting mother, painted it as a noble action. 'Judd's not gonna tolerate no sister of his hangin' out with no Mexican.' I didn't have the cojones to tell her it was over drug money. Judd and I were friends on this trip because we were the two older kids, I was sixteen and he was eighteen. I was overlooking the fact that Judd had been spending time with Laura since before he burned my hand in the park that night. I knew this because, after my acid high wore off, I remembered that she'd been wearing a bracelet I'd given him. Truth was, I was relieved he'd lost interest in me.

Nicole followed us to our tipi with clear intentions. I admired her tenacity and I did have reason to let her sleep in there with us, despite being mad at her. He let her chirp for a few minutes before grabbing her by her ponytail and leading her out the flap. I let her go. Instead I liked the idea that he and I were equals now, brother and sister, instead of him being lord and master, a role he naturally assumed as the boyfriend. I'd read an article about misogynists and made the mistake of sharing what I'd learned with Shelly one afternoon. She didn't want to hear that her son had a dysfunctional and sometimes violent need to control the women he dated, even harbored a bit of hate for females in general, all stemming back to mommy issues. No, she didn't want to hear that at all.

I organized our gear inside, and Judd set up a hammock by our fire pit. "I think I'm gonna sleep in it tonight."

"Really?" I asked, crinkling my nose. I didn't imagine a hammock would be very comfortable to sleep in.

"Yeah, there's only the one bed in there." He tightened a tether. "You can have it."

I guess it made sense, I hadn't really thought of how we'd work it. Honestly, I figured we'd share the surprisingly comfortable foam-topped camping palette in our own sleeping bags. This was an unexpected role reversal, I was the queen in the chamber, and he was my posted guard. I could get used to this.

He smiled big, and said, "Let's cruise the campground tonight, mom won't care." Before I could answer, he whispered, "Wherever you are, find me before dinner," as we exited.

In the neighboring tipi yard, Jason shouted

"Heeeeyyy!" at something and Shelly walked up on him and slapped his face so hard I thought I heard something crack. He bawled as loud as he'd shouted and Judd strode over, hovering over him until he dropped to his knees in the dirt. Jason stayed down and folded over on himself, rocking and sobbing. Twenty minutes of the rest of us unpacking went by before the boy got up and slunk off to the restroom.

With the exception of Jason, whose face was claret red and streaked all over—and not just where his mom had struck him, we were all in good spirits. Shelly, our happy social secretary, let us know we'd have dinner at the café at six. I was playing go fish with Nicole while Nate gave us a detailed report of the area insect population, sometimes bringing smooshed samples on the end of his stick to illustrate. Jason sat in Judd's hammock, by some miracle allowance, and glowered. I let Nicole win the last of three card games, and when I popped into the tipi at five-fifteen, I found out what Judd's secret plan was.

"Wanna fry?" He was seated on the edge of the bed palette tearing at something. I smelled pot.

"I don't really like pot that much," I said.

"No, no… Ugh, you're so dumb." He shook his head and held up a tiny baggie. "You wanna trip around the campground tonight." It was a statement, not a question. "Close your eyes, stick out your tongue."

I did.

"And… the cool thing is that it hits you differently if you dose right before a meal." He sold it like the final fantastic design feature on a line of kitchen storage products.

It sounded like we were in for a fun night; dinner, then back to the tipis for family time, then Judd and I had full freedom to prowl the campground on a warm spring night. It was probably a good idea that I only took one hit this time. The night at the bridge I'd taken two, and I didn't end up having a very good time. It was scary, and exhausting. My jaw, wrists, and shoulders were sore the following evening, and I had marks in the palms of my hands that I'd hoped were from my own fingernails, though the pattern wasn't quite a match. It was a horror movie at times, but this time I looked forward to getting the fantasy movie experience. I wanted the unicorns and starshine they promised, not spiders, or clowns whispering 'foresee dew.'

After dinner I realized I couldn't stand to listen to Shelly's voice. Outside the tipis I sat away from the group, and it occurred to me that I didn't remember walking back. And her voice. Her voice sounded like… I don't know what, but I couldn't stand it. Luckily nobody was talking to me, because I couldn't speak. Judd managed the fire over which the kids were messing up s'mores, and kept Shelly's attention telling her about his new job as a pork-sift operator. Judd's voice sounded like tumbling boulders, but it was much better than Shelly's. Her voice sounded like... It was like me scraping my finger through the dry stone dust on the side mirror of Ted's truck.

We're gonna walk up to the ghost town." I heard Judd say, and I got up from the picnic table and had an epiphany. Of course! That was the problem. Shelly's voice would have sounded normal if I'd just been looking at her while she was talking. I walked the long way around the picnic table, and straight to our tipi. I think I said, 'I'm getting my sweatshirt.'

I felt much better inside the tipi, and I turned on the camping lamp Judd had rigged. It cast a blue glittery light in the rounded space, and convinced me my unicorns were on their way. I headed toward my backpack and it grew immense in my sight until I touched it, then it grew much smaller as I fished inside for my sweatshirt.

We headed for the ghost town by way of the pool. He told me his work story too, about the forklift operator who'd given notice, and was tasked with training Judd during his final two weeks as his replacement. "I like the guy," he confided. "He's a wetback, but he's all right... moving to Barstow, he told me."

The pool area had been improved; there was a seven-foot-tall dark wood fence replacing the ugly old chain link, and an observation tower had been erected since the last time I'd been there. Standing almost two stories high and constructed of dark wood to match the fence, it was too tall and too decorative to be a lifeguard stand. Nobody else was there, and the pool area was still technically open another forty-five minutes. We helped ourselves to the view from the tower. The landscaping lights looked like a sci-fi movie effect, they threw brilliant pink and aqua chevrons around themselves like little frozen fire dancers. And the glow of the pool's surface looked like the best textured and softest trampoline I'd ever seen, even the world's biggest trampoline, but clearly designed and fabricated by a technologically superior alien race. If he hadn't instructed me to keep low in the tower, I would have loved to have jumped on that tram-pool-ine.

"Are you feeling it?" he asked.

I was feeling meat in my shirt and it turned out to be his hands groping me. He was sitting on an overturned bucket, and I was seated on the deck in front of him. All I could do was look at the lights. I couldn't move, and the meat became almost unbearably uncomfortable. The pink and green chevrons were my favorite things, and I wished I could use one to stab at his paws so he'd get them off my breasts. But I couldn't move.

Climbing out of the tower was indescribable fun, especially since it got his damn hands off me, and put me in semi-charge of my own person once again.

The ghost town was just that, but the floodlights were on, and we ventured through the one breezeway between two of the storefronts to see if any treasures were hidden out back. The back alley, such as it was, resembled that of any roadside motel in a slasher flick, complete with ditched crates, tires, trash bags and other debris, but with no passage in either direction for the hilly upslope. Making our way back through we discovered something on a darkened window casing—the biggest cockroach I'd ever seen. Judd became fascinated and gently nudged it with a twig, making it move into better view. I kept my distance. I could see it just fine.

"These things hiss." He poked further and I heard what sounded more like a growl than a hiss. I wasn't as interested as he was, and I scooted past, out to the mouth of the board walkway. I watched, wondering why this, of all disgusting things, captivated him. He'd never been especially fascinated by nature before, and I hoped he wasn't thinking of collecting it as some vile trinket or keepsake of our expedition. "They're not poisonous." This fun fact didn't make me feel any better. I was relieved when he broke his trance, tossed the twig, and we headed back.

The light was still on in my tipi and it was chilly inside, as it was outside. Someone had left what must have been some s'mores on a paper plate on the bed, and the sight of them inspired a giggling fit I couldn't control. Judd shared my amusement when I showed him the mangled chocolate mess, then he shushed me, "Shut UP! My mom will come over here." He grabbed my elbow and pressed himself against the length of my arm, rubbing the crotch of his jeans on my wrist.

We were dead silent hoping not to hear stirrings from the other tipi. I couldn't deal with her confronting me this high, but I also thought the problem would be solved if he'd just retire to his hammock. Then I thought about the reality of being alone.

I pulled away from him and he said, "You done with your giggle game, girl?"

I ignored his question, and crawled away onto the bed. It was cold and I was beginning to feel like I had when interaction between us was one-sided and manipulative. Like when we'd broken up. I'd felt appropriately stung when I'd asked him why Laura had the bracelet and he'd confessed with zero remorse. His tone was so matter-of-fact that it took me a day or two to realize that I'd been cheated on, but mostly I was left wondering 'Why her?' as if it mattered.

"I gotta piss," he said and exited.

I used the opportunity to change into my sweats, hoping he wouldn't come back, but knowing he'd have to collect his sleeping bag, if nothing else. I dressed quickly and lied on the bed with my bag over me, unable to make the zipper work. I realized the light was still on and wished I'd turned it out as a signal that I didn't want company, but I couldn't get up now. I wanted to pretend to be asleep when he returned. I hoped it would discourage him. Of course I knew I wouldn't be sleeping that night. The apex of the tipi started to sway, but I didn't mind too much.

Judd came back with a lawn chair.

"It's cold out there." He unfolded the creaky chair, set it gingerly near our gear and took a seat. He wasn't smiling now. "Looks like you're gonna have to share." He said, kicking his sleeping bag so it rolled over to the bed. These tipis were big enough to sleep a dozen comfortably, but the floor was concrete and I couldn't ask him to sleep on the cold slab, mainly because I knew he'd refuse. I didn't say anything, and just hoped he was as disinterested as I was. He smoked a bowl and took off his pants. I kept looking at the inside of the cone above me and started to feel frozen, unable to move, not in control of my person in any way. There was a single star peeking through the opening at the top of the tipi.

He turned the light off and slid in next to me, "What'd I do?" he whispered in the blackness, "You're not speaking to me?" He didn't give me time to answer, he was kissing me, and the best I could do was float up to the opening. He didn't stop, and to my horror, before I could reach the starshine, I realized those goddam cockroaches—hundreds of those shiny hissing bastards—were crawling in and out of the opening in a tight, fractal formation. I was stuck having to float back down into my body, the body he was currently controlling. My eyes watered and I shook.

Chapter Six: American Girls

Shelly had been trying to recover from the backlash of the unfettered affection she'd lavished on me in the beginning, and overcompensating. She was inventing reasons to discipline me and almost certainly taking cues from Judd, in whose favor I no longer stood. She'd grounded me to the house for two weeks, even bringing her husband with her to deliver this verdict. I'd been packing for a sleepover at Hope's when Shelly and Carl came to the room.

I looked out the bus window and remembered the confrontation.

Judd had told her he'd seen my boyfriend's car at Hope's house. I'd started dating Jimmy to Judd's frustration, and it didn't take her long to come up with a reason to forbid me from seeing him. I was happy to hear he was still in town, I thought he'd already left for South San Francisco. I concealed my joy, which dissipated as she further explained she'd have to ground me for lying and planning a rendezvous. The permanently grey-faced Carl said about five words in support of his wife before reaching into his shirt pocket for a pack of smokes and slipping out of the room. I tried to tell her that I didn't know Jimmy would be there, but I didn't try very hard. I did *not* tell her that he was imminently relocating to South City to live with his grandmother. The more I processed the conversation—the dumb bad luck of Jimmy stopping by Hope's and Judd spotting him—the more I realized I wouldn't be carrying out Shelly's two-week sentence.

I'd pull in to the bus station in less than an hour, where Jimmy'd promised to meet me. I followed his own arrival by about five days. I'd served a little over a week of Shelly's detention, making plans, then I walked out the door just before dawn on a Tuesday, across suburban Sacramento to the bus station, and back to the bay. I didn't even close the door, afraid to wake Shelly or any of those kids who might make a big stink. They wouldn't even calculate the advantage to themselves if I no longer lived there, they'd just give me up out of spite. I didn't even want to think about what Judd might have done if he'd caught me trying to leave.

By all appearances, Jimmy's grandmother had been living in her walk-up in South City for about 119 years. A sweet, shriveled old woman, she called me "meha," held my face in her plump hands, chastised us for even thinking about pre-marital sex, only to immediately afterward say something warm and loving in Spanglish, making us laugh, if nervously. She fixed our dinner, and told me never to turn down a meal when I'm homeless. She said I was a welcome guest in her home for exactly one night.

In the morning, Jimmy and I took the bus to where he had an interview at a grocery store. We talked about the night of the intended sleepover, trying to straighten it out.

"Hope said you were coming over, I just wanted to say goodbye," he explained. "I didn't mean for all this to happen."

I assured him I wasn't there just because he was, despite the fact that he and I had talked about doing exactly this when we first started dating. I guess he'd thought he was the only serious one, or that it was all just romantic teenage babble. We got off the bus and walked a couple blocks. "What are you going to do?" He asked.

"I've got friends in San Mateo," I said.

And your family, right? Your mom?" he tried to confirm.

"No, she's in North Beach."

He stopped in front of the store and grabbed my arm. "Why didn't you call her?"

"She gave up all rights, last year, in a courtroom," I said. "When I was in the foster home."

He looked confused, and I realized that it would be confusing to someone who didn't know the whole story. Once I'd moved into Shelly's home, paperwork had to be filed, court dates scheduled. I was in the courtroom the day she'd waived her parental rights, though I didn't know what it meant. I'd thought it was a formality—something we had to do, however counter-intuitive, for legal purposes, before I could go back to live with her. But the reality had crystallized over the months. Besides, she lived in a one-room apartment with a retired sailor.

He looked at the store, shoppers coming and going. "I don't know how long I'll be."

"I'll wait." I moved around to the shaded side of the store and we looked at each other. He turned and walked through the sliding door.

I watched the shoppers come and go. I looked through my duffel bag at the things inside; my clothes, a wooden puzzle box, my diary, colored pencils, curling iron and other beauty items, a torn book of crosswords I'd stolen from a doctor's waiting room back in Sacramento, and my wallet. I sat on the concrete parking lump and the cool morning got warmer.

An hour later, he came back out, pinning a plastic tag to his shirt bearing his name in blue and white labelmaker tape. It was crooked. "I'm starting training today, right now."

"I can wait."

"I'll probably be here until at least four."

I looked down at my bag, and at the concrete lump

and said, "That's okay."

He looked at me in a few seconds of silence, and sighed. "Okay," he said, and disappeared once more through the sliding glass.

I was looking forward to going back, though I wasn't sure whom I'd find. I hadn't called anyone before I left. I was excited at the idea of finding some of my old friends and introducing them to Jimmy, even though we weren't really together anymore. I wanted to call Gram, I had a feeling she would be happy to talk to me. The last time I'd spoken to her, she was very warm, not terse at all, about anything. She didn't seem to resent me at that point, so I made a plan to talk to her before too many days passed. I assumed the state would get in touch with her, tell her that I had run away, and I didn't want her to worry. It occurred to me that now that Jimmy had a job, maybe he could get an apartment.

I waited in the afternoon sun and counted my cash. Seventy-eight dollars and some change. I'd cashed two savings bonds before I left for just a bit more than their face value each. Even if Jimmy did get an apartment, it would be a while. I'd have to stay somewhere in the meantime. I needed to call Jamie. I didn't expect to stay with him, but he knew people. I'd head to the mall and call him from there. Plus I was bound to run into someone there. I'd only been gone a year and I was sure they would all still be there.

I bothered a stranger for the time—it was ten after two. I wanted to get to the mall by 3:00. I couldn't wait for Jimmy, he'd have to come down on one of his days off. I got up and dusted off my ass, flinging my duffel over my shoulder. I found a clerk inside.

"Can I talk to Jimmy real quick?" I think I startled her, and she gave me a sour look, like I'd thrown up on her.

"Who?" she asked.

"Jimmy, just started here today," I begged as she knocked on a locked door with a darkened mirror set into the top half. "Mexican guy, white shirt, skinny black tie." I held my hand up to indicate he was about an inch taller than I was.

"I don't know him," she said to the door. A corpulent bald man opened it and she questioned him as he dabbed perspiration from his brow.

"We don't have anyone here by the name of Jimmy." He said with a pleasant smile. The clerk slipped into the office and the door glided shut.

It was a small mart, no more than four check stands. I was surprised they hadn't met him yet. He'd been there almost four hours. I couldn't wait, I had to catch the bus. I bought a coke and did the best I could to pass the message along to a clearly confused checker. "If you see Jimmy, tell him I'll call him in a few days."

"I don't know anyone named Jimmy," she said in a

valley girl tone.

"He's new, you'll probably meet him later." I took one last look around the store and left for the bus stop.

★★★

The pizza place was empty, which was good. It meant that the walkers hadn't gotten there yet. I waited in the atrium to catch anyone who might slide in the mall doors. I recognized a guy named Ben who was a freshman when I left. He was with three girls I didn't know. Some others came, and a few filed in to our corner of the pizza place. After a while I went back in to make sure none of my friends had come through the other door. By almost four, there was no one who'd recognize me, or care that I was back.

I walked the length of the mall, south to north as Jamie and I had done a hundred times, and bought some fries at the food court. I watched an impossibly thin girl wearing blue spandex pants, black high-heeled suede boots with fringe up the sides and a tied-at-the waist men's flannel shirt hanging off one shoulder revealing the inward curve that dips into the underarm and above where her little breast would start. I ate my greasy fries out of a paper cup, messy with ketchup, and watched her buy some nachos, flirting with the guy at the register throughout the process. Did she want jalapeños? Yes, then no, then giggle, then yes. He, at no more than fourteen, grinned wide, probably envisioning sucking a jalapeño slice out of her belly button and maybe a drizzle of cheese sauce off her neck. She had straight black hair to her waist, and bangs sprayed a half-mile high. She was beautiful. I watched her walk away with her nachos, and slip into a molded orange swivel seat at a table with guy in a blue t-shirt, the exact same blue as her spandex pants, with the name "Maverick" on it among red and white stripes over a white star.

It was Danny.

He saw me, and half waved-half saluted. I waved back. He continued to talk to Ms. Mall Bangs and I drowned my disappointment in ketchup. I thought he'd be more excited to see me. I'd hoped someone would be happy about my return. I was thinking I might have to contact Gram sooner than I'd planned when Danny took the seat opposite me.

"Hey, hey! Where've you been?" He was smiling big, and he flipped his blond feathery hair back. "Sheryl said you moved to Stockton?" The question of it pertained to the moving, not whether or not he'd gotten the right location.

"Not quite, but yeah…" I said. I looked over to the other table and found Ms. Mall Bangs nowhere in sight. I turned on the charm. "But I'm back now," I said with a smile and a lilt. "Except I don't really have anywhere to go." I delivered this line with a pout, and dug into my duffel bag for effect, and fishing for my diary.

"Aah, on the streets, huh?"

"Yeah, does Sheryl still have the same number?" I asked.

"Yep, I think she and her dad still live in that same place. We broke up."

"Oh." I thought about Ms. Mall Bangs. "Was that your girlfriend?"

He looked over his shoulder. "Nah! She's just a chick I know."

I flipped to the back of my diary to verify the non-crossed out version of Sheryl's phone number. "4-2-9-1?"

"Yup, Sheryl's number? Yup, that's it?" He confirmed the last four. "Hey, whaddya doin' tonight?" he asked with a smirk.

"Nothing in particular." Which meant, I had no plans and *please, oh please* invite me somewhere—which he did. Being homeless was a lot of work. I had only a short time to figure out how to please whomever was letting me stay. Come to think about it, that was the case even when I wasn't homeless. I had to suss out the new rules while trying to deconstruct how I'd gotten it wrong at the previous address. I didn't know much, but I did know that not all charitable offers to street kids were good, like Jimmy's grandmother. Afterschool Specials and PSAs had taught me that much. And it scared me to imagine what a sketchy offer could entail. Danny's offer superseded calling Sheryl for the time being. Luckily, it was a good offer.

✱✱✱

Danny's parents were out of town and a group of us hung out at their house in the hills that night—three guys and one other girl, none of whom I knew. I think they were other rich kids, and they really only talked to each other while Danny almost exclusively talked to me, except when he was telling the guests where the alcohol was, and that they had to smoke outside.

Danny and I wandered into a big yellow kitchen and I took a stool at the island. He handed me a bottle. "You know that guy Rob, right?" He asked as I took a pull of tequila.

"Yeah!" I'd almost forgotten about him. "What about him?"

"He and that dude Jamie are staying at an apartment off Fiesta. I get coke from their roommate."

That made me happy. "Can I get their number?" I was elated to hear Jamie wasn't living at home.

He set a couple shot glasses on the tile and reached into the fridge for a lime. "We need salt," he said, cutting wedges.

"What's Jamie's number?" I asked again.

"Oh, I can't give it out." He fashioned a shot and reached long across the counter for the salt shaker, leaving his feet planted. I became distracted when his t-shirt pulled up a bit revealing his side above the line of his jeans and stretched tight around the ripples on his back and shoulder. Danny was just over six feet tall, and lean.

We drank two more shots chased with beer, and he gave me the tour. The back patio area was under construction, right off the room he said I could sleep in. I dropped my bag there. He showed me the master suite and its oversized spa tub. One of the other guys was asleep on Danny's parents' bed, Danny claimed him as a childhood friend.

The remaining five of us ended up back at the kitchen island playing quarters with juice glasses of beer and shot glasses of tequila. One of the guys had an accent, Russian I think, and was certainly not high school age. I kept thinking about Sheryl's accurate number in my diary.

✳✳✳

I woke up on the bed in the room Danny had allotted to me, in my long, lime green sleeping shirt with a sparkly shooting star on the front of it. I remembered the other girl—I think her name was Catherine, or Katrina—leaving the game of quarters to line up some coke at the nearby kitchen table. I remembered turning on the hot water tap in the spa tub, and turning it off. I remembered being outside, on the front lawn barefoot, and that was about it. I started taking inventory of the present. The bedroom door was closed, and there were workers outside the glass slider.

It seemed important for me to jump up and get dressed, a little node of stark fear irritated my gullet, likely a product of waking up in nothing but my night shirt with four guys in the house, and not remembering getting undressed. I spotted the clothes I'd been wearing the night before as I pulled clean ones out of my bag. A pink and black off the shoulder sweatshirt and Jordache jeans would be just fine for the overcast morning. Last night's pegged jeans with the zippers up the ankles were as dirty as if I'd been wearing them for two days, which I had. I'd slept in them the night before I left Sacramento. I wadded them up with the Aerosmith baseball jersey and noticed the zippers were undone. I had a flash of Cathrina unzipping them and I felt light-headed. I had another flash of her looking at me intimately or maybe intensely, but I think I would have remembered hooking up with her. I definitely remembered us laughing together. That was real. Come to think of it, that was all she said. Other than laughter, she didn't utter a single word all night. Nothing but the occasional chortle from under her tawny brown bob cut and a constant smile across her cream-complected face. And that one moment of hearty laughter from the both of us—her imperfect teeth shining behind plum lips. That I remember, though I don't know what we were laughing at. I found my bra and panties, expecting even more clues in flashes. Nothing. I was sure that if she and I had done anything, it was no more than her helping out a drunken sister.

I stuffed everything into my duffel and peeked out into the hallway. I headed for the bathroom. I was pleased to find nothing seriously wrong with the girl in the mirror. An ornate clock on the towel organizer showed it was just after 9 am. Funny, I hadn't noticed a clock in the guest room. I chuckled as I thought someone had stolen it, though I hoped I wouldn't be blamed. Then I thought maybe Cathrina—weird, silent, intense Cathrina might have... OH FUCK!

I slammed my bag on to the sink-top and threw the zipper open, desperate to find my wallet. It wasn't there. No, no, no, no, oh fuck!

I pulled everything out, and found my diary. I flipped through it in case I'd written in it, or taken down a number, squashed a daisy, hidden some cash, left myself a note—anything. There was nothing new among its pages. I almost started crying, and I looked at my things scattered among the white shag of the bathroom rug and across the aqua tile. I started all over again, throwing my things into new piles and wondering which assholes were still in the house. My wallet fell out of a fistful of clothes and I yanked it open, to find it thankfully still stuffed with my small fortune. I took the most relieved pee in history while separating the single cash stash into three smaller accounts using my diary and the puzzle box.

Danny was in the kitchen having a fruit roll-up with coffee. "Hey, wanna go get some breakfast before we head over to Sheryl's?"

I didn't know how to answer that question, I didn't realize we were meeting up with Sheryl. "What?" I asked, feeling a bit hungry.

"Yeah, she called back last night after you passed out." He said it so matter-of-factly, but I still didn't want to ask him what happened. "Her dad said you could stay there for a month, figure shit out."

"Oh, that's totally awesome!" I started to remember calling Sheryl, and I was so relieved to have a month of roof over my head. Of course, I was frustrated that I couldn't remember so much of what happened, or what I'd said to Sheryl. I had to figure out a sneaky way to get the info.

Danny jumped up from his counter stool and came at me. He scooped me up in a tight hug and kissed my neck, giving my butt a squeeze in the process. My heart stepped up the pace and I had a flash, upon smelling him—his cologne, his smokiness, his breath—of us making out. So... I hadn't hooked up with Catherina, or whatever the hell her name was, I'd made out with Danny. This frustrated me. I'd always liked him, and I thought we'd have made a cuter couple than he and Sheryl, but I didn't want my first encounter with him to be the result of too much tequila.

"I'm gonna take a shit then we'll go!" he said and strode off, obviously in a good mood.

And now we were leaving, and I hadn't even showered, and I was going to stay with Sheryl—his ex. I hoped to gawd we hadn't had sex.

I poured a cup of coffee and looked around at the modest mess, trying to glean more clues. I tried to find any reason to assume we hadn't had sex; I was in the guest room with the door shut, I had my nightshirt on, I was on top of the covers, I didn't see a condom wrapper, I didn't wake up next to him, I didn't feel anything... I didn't remember it! It looked like I was going to have to engineer the perfect breakfast conversation.

✦✦✦

Sheryl's dad gave me 30 days, and she and I were in charge of keeping the apartment clean. They, in fact, did not live in the same place, a detail that sent Danny and me on an unnecessary trip across the water. When we arrived at the proper destination, Sheryl and Danny caught up for twenty minutes or so. They'd been together over two years and had enough of their own inside jokes to make me feel like odd-girl-out yet again. On the drive over he kept grabbing my hand. At the pay phone, when we called Sheryl to find out where she really lived, he put his arm around my neck and pulled me into him kissing my forehead. But here at Sheryl's kitchen table, his body language was different, I couldn't tell if he was trying to preserve my feelings or hers.

When they wrapped up their chat and hugged goodbye he looked at me, keys in hand. "You coming down?" I looked at her and she said she'd be in her room and told me not to lock myself out.

Down at his car, he pulled me in with deep kisses. "I didn't want to say anything in front of Sheryl, but your buddy Rob and my coke dealer live right around the corner from here."

"But, doesn't she do coke?"

"Nope," he said. "She doesn't do anything anymore."

"Oh, that's cool." I wondered if she would admonish me for last night's debauchery and I felt heavy guilt. But I also noted that she looked great, happy and healthy, like women look when they're pregnant.

"So, let's do something soon." He looked at me, arms wrapped tight around me, like he wasn't sure if last night was just a fleeting moment, and if it was, as if he really wanted at least one more. "My parents are out of town a lot, and you won't have to worry about coming back here after drinking."

"Yeah. You have my number," I reminded him with a touch of amusement and irony. Another kiss and I was certain we hadn't had sex. He pulled away and headed out.

Sheryl's room had a sliding glass door to a balcony that overlooked the interchange of the highway that went to the coast, and the one that went to Los Angeles. The vista reminded me of a Tom Petty song.

"This is my room, and you could crash in the living room, but I think it's better if we just share this room, if you're okay with that." She explained that it was a small apartment, and her dad was still working graveyard. We'd have to be quiet during the day while he slept, and it was easier for us to consolidate into her room for our living space.

"No problem," I said. She had a queen bed, more than big enough for the two of us.

"I cleared out a drawer in my dresser for you." She chirped, and hopped up out of her desk chair to yank it open. "Ta-daaaaa!" she chimed.

That evening while her dad drank his coffee, we sat in her room and talked about the past year. She was finishing up school a few months early and working as a part-time office clerk. They said they'd make her full-time once she graduated, and she wanted the full-time pay now. She wasn't looking to move out, but she did want a car.

She explained that she'd stopped smoking pot, and didn't drink either. "Yeah, it's a little awkward having a Jack and coke in the evening when my dad is just getting ready to go to work, so I just don't drink." She smiled. "And I just don't have time to be stoned anymore, not with what I've got going on."

"Oh, so you didn't go to AA or anything," I said.

"No, it's just not convenient, and I save money." She shrugged. "My dad'll have a drink or two on his nights off if he goes out, but not much. It messes up his sleeping schedule."

I thought about that, and remembered my mom when she had been working graveyard at a hotel. I would come home from school to empty bottles in the living room and her in an emotional state. I once found her lying in bed, weeping and unable to move. She'd tripped over the cat and broken her arm in two places.

"Hey! Did you and Danny… y'know?" She grinned and put her left index finger through the "O" formed by the thumb and index finger of her right hand.

I looked at her with a blank stare.

"I remember his always being so quiet," she said. "Our first few times, I thought he wasn't enjoying it." She lit a cigarette, and crossed to the sliding glass door to crack it open. "At least he always made me come."

I still couldn't answer. I couldn't visualize me and Danny in the act, but I certainly could picture the two of them, thanks to her revelation. I shook it off.

"Honestly, I'm not sure!" I flopped forward from my seated position on her bed and buried my face in my hands.

"What?!" she said.

"I don't think we did it, but I don't know for sure." I sat up groaning and joined her for a smoke.

She laughed, and said, "Uh oh... What the hell were you guys drinking?"

"Tequila."

"Oh, SHIT!" She was just a little too amused. Then she got serious.

"You need to ask him." She thought a moment, then said, "Or wait for your next period."

I spoke up. "No, that's just it." I was sure of myself. "I would never have let him do it without protection."

"Really?"

"Yes. Drunk or not, I don't care."

She said, "Or just..."

"—Well, yeah. Or that." I gave it a moment's thought. "I would do that, but I didn't."

She frowned and asked, "How do you know?"

"Well, for one thing, my jaw would be sore."

"Oh yeah." She put out her cigarette, and said, "Well, you still have to ask him." I supposed she was right. "Or..." she said, "I'll ask him!"

"—Yeah!" I adored her elegant solution, as well as her eagerness to carry it out.

"Are you guys going to go out again?"

"I think so. He said he wanted me to come over when his parents are out of town again." I was giddy at both prospects.

"Well, when he calls, I'll answer." She looked up surprised, and I turned to see her dad in the doorway. "Hey dad!" she said with genuine affection.

"Good evening, ladies," He was smallish but fit, and a charmingly balding man. "Hi, Connie, nice to see you again. Welcome to Chez Keller."

"Thanks," I said, through a nervous grin.

She crossed the room to hug him. "We weren't too loud earlier, were we?"

"Nope. I was in dreamland," he answered. "I'm off to the salt mines, you two have a good night."

"You too, daddy, love you."

"G'night, Mr. Keller." I felt like an imp. She smiled after him down the hall then came back and peeled off her shirt.

"Holy shit, how long was he standing there?" I asked.

She extracted a t-shirt and night shorts from the dresser, and unzipped her mini-skirt. "Oh, he doesn't care. He's not stupid, he knows we're women."

After the best shower I could remember, I found my new roommate in the living room, smoking by the open slider, and watching Night Court. Apparently, her father's room was the only one without a balcony overlooking the freeways. A wee red light was blinking on the answering machine by the apartment's front door, and I leaned in to look at the display. There was a digital "2" in the window.

"Danny didn't call," she said. That's the one from you last night, and one from dad's dentist."

"One from me?" I asked. Again, I had to come out straight with her. "I was so drunk when I talked to you, I barely remember it."

"Really? You didn't sound drunk."

"What did I say?"

"You just said you were at Danny's and I should call you back… which I did."

I knew this was a good opportunity to piece some of the evening together so I prodded further. "What time was it?"

She knew what I was getting at and didn't mind providing answers, she turned off the TV. Like I said, she was generous like that. "You called me at 7:30, I called you back at, like, 8:00." She drew a glass of water in the kitchenette and said, "Do you want anything, are you hungry?"

"Hell yes!" I went in and was thrilled to make a bologna sandwich with mayo on white bread, and even happier to scarf it down over the sink with a cup of milk. "I have some grocery money, if you want to tell me what your dad likes. We can go to the store tomorrow."

"Sure," she said. "I have to work in the morning, but when I get home."

"So," I asked through a mouthful of sandwich, "you talked to Danny after I went to bed?"

She looked at me and leaned on the sink. "You don't remember anything, do you?" I shook my head. "We talked for a half hour. You told me what was going on, and asked if you could stay here." I was dismayed by my own blatant cry for charity. Another flash of memory came as a jubilant me getting off the phone with her and celebrating, at the game of quarters, potential receipt of a crash pad. She went on as she led us out of the kitchenette to bed. "You told me you'd only had pancakes and fries to eat all day. Dude, that's not a good diet to follow up with tequila and blow."

I jumped when she said that, and felt queasy. I didn't think I'd done any coke.

We settled in under the covers and I felt better, even if I was in the same green nightshirt I'd woken up in that morning.

Sheryl turned out the light and said after a moment in the dark, "You should tell me more about Judd, and that family when you're ready."

I was too tired to bug her anymore, and I laid there in the dark wondering how much I'd told her about Judd and Shelly.

Danny's parents were gone the following weekend and, as planned, I spent the night with him… and his damn childhood friend again. There was more drinking, of course, but I stayed away from any distilled spirits and stuck with beer. There was no coke around this time, and he told me that I hadn't done any coke that first night either, which was a relief. After his friend passed out again, Danny and I had the alone time to consummate what we hadn't before. Actually, it scored points with me that he hadn't taken advantage of me. He promptly declared us boyfriend and girlfriend and I went along with it. It was okay by me if things moved forward at a good clip. Danny was eighteen and done with school, even if it was by way of dropping out during his senior year. He was looking at getting an apartment.

We rode around on Danny's rebuilt motorcycle without helmets, and rode to where Jamie and Rob were staying one afternoon the week before Easter. I found Jamie changed, not the goofy boy he'd been before, but reserved and distant. I had called him once from Sacramento, and Judd had made a big stink about it, so it was the one and only call I'd made to my best friend over the year. If he was pissed at me, he didn't say so.

He didn't mention it, instead we talked about the present. He couldn't stay at that apartment much longer, and his impending homelessness startled me more than it did him. By all appearances, Jamie was just fine. He primped his grown-out, layered, sandy hair in the mirror without looking at me and said, "I'm not sure what I'm gonna do now, I'm about to graduate." He was indifferent, then he finished, "I'm thinking I'll go to L.A."

I was surprised to hear this, but it seemed congruous enough.

"Who with?" I asked.

"Nobody." He stepped away from the bathroom vanity to push by me into the apartment's hallway then retraced his steps back when he saw Rob and Danny in the living room. He looked at me. "What about you. What are you going to do?"

"I don't know." I didn't tell him I was hoping I'd be able to live with Gram. I'd seen her once. She called me and said that a bird had gotten into her closet, and she asked if I could come over. Danny and I'd motorbiked over and Danny was able to rescue the bird. It was the first time I'd seen her new house, and I wanted to live there with her. I didn't for a minute believe the odds of her inviting me to stay were in my favor. I answered Jamie again, "I don't really know."

"Come with me if you want," he said. "Imma hitchhike. And it's pretty easy to live on the streets until you can hook up with people."

I was thrilled at his offer, frightened at the idea, and put off that it seemed like nothing more than an afterthought. Still, it was an option.

✸✸✸

Sheryl and I stayed up late some nights playing

poker for the peanut butter and cheese crackers I'd bring home from the mini-mart where I cashiered. For some reason, the owner, a kind, widowed Iranian man, let me have all the cheese and peanut butter cracker packets I wanted. I'd bought her flowers, a bouquet of things bright red and deep violet to show my appreciation for sharing her space. One night as we lied in bed, she said with mirth, "Hey, I just read somewhere that red and purple are royal colors!" She rolled on to her right side and hoisted her left leg to rest bent-kneed on top of the bedspread. She hugged a pillow and looked at me with a smile reflected in her brown eyes as she said, "I've never had a boyfriend send me royal flowers. Or flowers that made me feel like royalty."

"Yeah, guys don't think about that stuff, I guess." Her flirty tone was cute, and it always so nicely offset her usual serious and responsible manner, just like her milky skin offset her jet-black hair. It was amazing that this girl, who looked like she could have Native American ancestry could live in California, lay her lovely bikini body by the pool as often as any other California girl did, and maintain such an alabaster complexion with only a few well-placed freckles.

"Danny was a good boyfriend," she countered. "He gave me a pretty watch, and he took me to prom, bought me a corsage." She rolled onto her back to look at the popcorn ceiling. "But I don't remember him ever giving me flowers…"

She was talking about my guy, but I didn't care. I was glad the competition had stopped—the constant, inherent competition among very young women that propped up patriarchy. I wasn't even sure at what point I'd noticed it, but it was societal. It seemed designed to keep women fractured and in doubt, harping over hair color and strappy shoes, and men in positions of advantage, most regrettably, the wrong men. Some women embraced it, but not Sheryl. I was glad of that, because I'd become tired of it—tired of living by something that only makes women petty and self-obsessed.

"You and him are hanging out a lot," she said.

"Yeah."

She switched gears. "Hey, I hope you're not going to be here all by yourself Sunday. I would be sad if you were." She was sincere. " 'Cause you know, we'll be at my aunt's."

"I know."

"And my dad has to work that night, so he'll want to come home and lay down."

"That's okay, I'll be at my Gram's," I lied. I had less a week to try to figure out where to spend Easter Sunday. I didn't want to be there at her apartment. I really didn't care about Easter, I had bigger things on my mind, but I didn't want to push the envelope on how much neediness she and her dad could bear. Danny was obligated to his mom's dinner arrangements, but said he could meet me in the evening. I'd sit in the park all day if I had to.

"Oh good! I didn't know you'd talked to her. I'm so happy for you!" Her joy may have been premature, I could probably secure an Easter invite from the family, but I didn't hope to find my next address in it. With that being my immediate agenda, I didn't know what there was to socialize over dinner about.

"Don't forget, Sunday is your vacuuming and dusting day," she reminded.

"Oh yeah, I'll do it before I go." I promised.

The following day I called Mindy but found only Mary at home. Mindy was busy with school, work, and playing Magenta in The Rocky Horror Picture Show but Mary insisted on seeing me. I invited her over and we sat in Sheryl's room, talking about things that seemed quite important to her. She wore the same flippy brown wig, or a similar one, and still tipped her head and smiled as she told me how proud she was of Mindy. She asked me about the foster home, and I proffered short, guarded answers. I didn't trust her entirely because I couldn't figure out why she was there. I usually just didn't trust men, but I knew exactly why that was. I wasn't sure why I didn't trust her, but maybe it was because she and Bob and Ted and my mom had once been close friends. I wasn't conscious of it at the time, but the strange advantage to moving from home to home was getting further and further from Ted. Of course another way to parse that is that being in 'survival mode,' not having any permanence also didn't give me any time to think much about him or his effect on me as a girl, as a person, as a woman. But now someone with only one degree of separation from him was here chit-chatting with me from a simple phone call after almost four years of non-contact. And anyway, I hadn't called to connect with her, had I? I couldn't figure her motivation, until she mentioned my mom.

"When was the last time you spoke to your mom?" she asked.

"I called her at Christmas," I said. "She was at the Columbus."

"The Columbus?" She tipped her head so far to the left I thought her wig might slip.

"It's a bar. In North Beach," I said. "That's where I can usually call her. Haven't you talked to her?" I asked.

"Nope. She was pissed at me for taking you to Capitola." She smiled and cocked her eyebrows, they disappeared up under the bangs of the wig. "You remember the day we went to beach with my in-laws, right?"

"Yeah, it was fun." I remembered it well. On the way back we'd stopped at a resort's lounge off the highway and had cocktails. I had a Shirley Temple, and sat with the grown-ups while Mindy and her cousin played in the woods outside. It was a sweet little recollection. For a moment, it was nice to remember back to before everything went sideways.

"She was supposed to pick you up that Sunday morning," Mary continued. "She didn't show up."

"Oh, yeah."

"She didn't show up because she was in the city doing heroin with some people."

"Oh."

"Have you ever done heroin?" she asked.

"No."

She rattled off a list of narcotics and I shook my head to all of them.

"Drugs are very dangerous," she said. "Don't do any of them. There's no point. If you haven't already tried them, just stay away from them. You don't want to go down that road. Grass isn't so bad, but don't fool around with the heavy stuff."

I thought she was being silly. I didn't know anyone who did any of those things. She laughed "Oh dear," in a singsong way and said, "your mother and I used to smoke grass when you girls were little. We had so much fun." She giggled more and snorted, "If I drank beer, I'd always get in trouble. Bob didn't like it when I drank." She snapped to attention and asked me what time it was. Before I could answer, she saw the clock on Sheryl's nightstand. "I have to go now, I'm sorry." She stood and looked around almost wild-eyed. Then she looked at me and tipped. "Ooohh, we were having such a nice conversation, but I have to get home." I showed her out as quietly as I could past Sheryl's dad's door, and she promised to tell Mindy I'd called.

★★★

To my surprise, Auntie Elyse turned out to be my contact for Easter dinner. She'd gotten a commitment from my mom, and she insisted I come too, even offering to pick me up.

Before dinner, Lawrence talked about a parishioner who'd been acting odd at the morning's prayer service. He said one of his favorite confidantes, an elderly black woman who was always accompanied by her large extended family had leaned into him, pointing and whispering that the old guy was "stoned." He told it to us in the same hushed tone she would have used. I asked him what he meant, and he clarified that the fellow had come to church drunk. I found the use of the term to broadly cover any brand of intoxication charming and folksy. Will rolled his eyes.

My mom and I sat outside at the umbrella table and talked about everything but the elephant. She'd taken the train down from the city and she talked about her friends who had names like Dino and Paulie. I told her about Sheryl—about how pretty she was, and about her dad. I didn't tell her about our arrangement's impending terminus, and she didn't ask about the foster home. I tried to picture her doing the things Ted and Mary had said she'd done, but she didn't look like the people in the PSAs. She just looked like my mom.

Will showed me around Gram's house leading us to the kitchen. He was full of smiles and in his usual talkative mood; and I loved that it was me he enjoyed talking to. He was funny, and we had a confidence that left the others out of the loop. He asked me about Sacramento, if I was glad to be out of there, then changed the subject before I could answer. "Hey, did I tell you I'm moving to Portland?" He reached under the sink and fished out a can of beer.

"Elyse told me," I said, thinking about Gram's guest room.

He up-ended the beer and buried the can in the trash back under the sink. "I bought a house! Can you believe it? I bought a house without having a job." He was elated. "Nobody gets to buy a house without having a job, Connie."

Gram called to Will from the living room.

No one spoke of anything important, it was all weather and current events—excluding politics—and other banal pleasantries. We stalked around the landscaped backyard looking for the eggs Will had stashed, while Gram and my mom tended a ham. The food was fine, and after dinner they cleared the dishes and talked amongst themselves.

I had nothing to contribute. I could only think of one thing—where was I going to live in thirteen days?

I went out to the back steps and cried. It blew over me like a zephyr as soon as I was alone. I bawled. I was scared at the thought of what seemed to be my only option, hitchhiking to Los Angeles with Jamie.

"Connie?" Gram poked her head out the French door.

I didn't answer her, just kept sobbing at the mercy of the release. And anyway, there was nothing to be gained by discussing it. I couldn't think of any reason to tell them I was going to L.A.

Will came out and plopped down next to me and put an arm around my shoulder. "Is it about your friend Sheryl?"

I didn't know what he thought it had to do with her. I wasn't sure how much he knew, I'd told only Elyse about the thirty-day agreement.

"You're getting kicked out, aren't you? he asked.

I corrected his interpretation of the situation. "Thirty days was the agreement," I said through a sob.

"Well honey, what are you going to do?" Gram asked. She accentuated the 'honey' part in a way that implied I should have somehow planned for this.

"I don't know." I whispered.

Will looked at her. "Mom—" His one word address

to Gram had some meaning to which I was not privy, and I heard her slip back into the house behind me. I wiped my face and took a staccato breath.

"You should come to Portland with me," Will said.

I couldn't think, but I knew better than to turn him down. "Okay." I said, as I tried to process what it meant, and thinking about Sheryl and Danny… and Jamie.

"I'm leaving next week." He hugged me. "We'll drive up in Lawrence's old truck."

Elyse appeared with a cup of water and a tissue box. "It'll be okay," she said.

Will chimed in, squeezing my shoulder and giving me a nudge. "She's going to live in Portland with me!"

I got up and looked at her as I dusted off my backside.

"Oh, okay." She looked puzzled. "That was fast."

"She's gotta go somewhere," Will said with a shrug.

We went inside, and she narrowed her eyes on me. "Don't you have to tell your roommate? She was kind enough to take you in."

Elyse's comment seemed incongruous and accusatory, and I didn't have time to unpack it. I was guilty of securing my next place to stay, I guess. I stepped past her without answering and sat down in one of the cane-backed dining chairs and gulped my water.

Lawrence, Gram, and my mom were directly across

in the living room, and Will and Elyse filed in. My mom appeared unaffected which I realized was common for her when we were all together. Anytime it was just the two of us, she'd tell me how much she admired Naval ships or fine art sketch work, or she'd confide in me how much she was put off by the president's lack of concern for the homeless and infirm. I also noticed for the first time that day that she was dressed like a man in jeans and a brown button down dress shirt. Not a hint of femininity. Elyse set the tissues in front of me, and I transferred them to the buffet behind me. Will disappeared down the hall to the bathroom.

"Feeling better?" Gram asked.

"Yeah—"

"She's going to Portland with Will," Elyse said.

Lawrence said, "Well, isn't that lovely."

Chapter Seven: Stumptown Elysium

I was in a dark, narrow passage that seemed like a passenger train for the bunks on one side. The bunks weren't stacked, they were end to end, and Sheryl popped up in one of them like someone undead in an open casket. 'Isn't this great?' she said. 'We can stay here together and never have to leave San Mateo!' I was pulling away or being pulled back and the dimness was getting redder, and I could hear her saying, 'It's our apartment. I promise it is.' Red faded to glittery blackness, and a seven-foot tall rabbit glided by making a stomping sound.

She'd been happy for me when I told her I was moving to Oregon to live with my other uncle. I hadn't gotten such an affectionate send-off from Danny. In fact, he'd stood me up that night after Easter dinner, left me loitering on the avenue. A few other men had offered me a ride under the April streetlights outside a pancake restaurant, but none of them were him. When I'd finally called his house, his mom said he was asleep. A few days later I caught up with him and before I could tell him I was leaving for Oregon, he fumbled over phrases like, 'can't see you for a while,' and 'not a good match,' so I didn't bother to tell him. Jamie's roommate George had taken me and some other people out to a wide-open, dry reservoir bed off the freeway to drink wine coolers under the stars— said it was my "going away party." I'd only met the guy the one time, and didn't know the others at all, but I assumed Jamie had set it up and would be along later. One of them was wearing a t-shirt with Judd's 'Death Before Dishonour' artwork screen-printed on it. It wasn't Judd's original work at all. He was a plagiarist and an infringer.

I'd drank with these people and talked about a new life, about possibilities. That was, I guess, the nice thing about being in that place that night with total strangers, there was no prologue, no burdensome expectations, only blank pages. Jamie never came.

The weird dream was an artifact of how genuinely sad Sheryl had been to see me go. Her sincerity even made me uncomfortable. Non-sexual affection baffled me. I missed her, but it was hard to hang on to friends over long distances, and hard to know how to store friendships since the next sea-change might find me right back in her 'hood.

I heard Will leave through the back door as I woke up, and I assumed that he was the stompy, giant rabbit in the dream. Oregon's May sun was kissing the roses outside my bedroom window while an afternoon breeze was slapping them around. His house was off a major thoroughfare in Southeast Portland and sat on a double lot. The house itself was small, no more than a thousand square feet as long as you counted the partially finished basement. There were two tiny bedrooms on the main floor and a converted attic. The double-sized yard contained some neat blackberry rows, a cherry tree, and a rickety tool shed. I wanted to make friends, I wanted to find a summer job, and eventually I needed to finish high school. Will had a good friend from the bay area in town who'd helped him find the house.

'What's in it for me?' was one of Will's go-to lines. Taking me in meant young men in and out of the house; I guess I was bait. A permanent member of the boys' club, Will was an accomplished hedonist and successful at rooting out the bi-curious who swilled beer and complained about girls who'd screwed them over. Sure, they were mostly straight guys as far as I knew, but they were just basic boys who liked a little beer, a little loud music, a little sumpin' sumpin'. I don't know enough about male sexuality to know if they were ready to experiment, or if he mostly convinced them with liquor and weed—or if it was a bit of both, but his conversion rate was pretty good, if he's to be believed. He was fun, and funny, and liked to laugh and loved to have fun, and I can almost remember the very day I'd decided I loved him. It was like picking out a sweater at a thrift store. I swore, on the spot, loyalty to my uncle. I needed an adult male

I could trust; and I had reason to believe he was as marginalized as I was. I'm pretty sure he also enjoyed having me around to do the housework he loathed. I didn't really mind.

I'd napped for over two hours before being jolted awake by the dream. I took a moment to appreciate that I'd been able to just… sleep… in the middle of the day. I'd always felt like I was on sentry duty, or like someone who still had some miles to travel. I wasn't sure how long I'd felt that way, but long enough to have gotten used to it.

The insecurity of semi-homelessness would follow me into my twenties. One Friday evening, I dropped in on a friend, and was astonished to find him napping. I peeked in the window of the house he rented before going to the door and saw him stretched out on his bed in the waning late afternoon light. In that moment I thought to myself, 'How can he just *sleep*?' as if he had no right to rest. For a while after that, it was the sentiment itself that perplexed me. Did I believe that some of us should have to toil every moment just to have the human basics, was his fifty-hour work week not enough? I had an expectation that he should be always alert, ready to take action against whomever might snatch away his place to live.

I got up, washed my face, and pulled back my curly hair. I'd given up on straightening it. I was blonde like everybody else in the family, but I was the only one with brown eyes. I looked in the mirror and saw a freckled girl of no discernible age. If I was to find a job or make some friends, it wasn't going to happen inside that house.

I walked out to the bus line and waited in the late afternoon sun. Traffic whipped past me and I tried to think of where Will might have gone. We'd been in Portland just shy of a week and his relationship with his friend was showing signs of strain, even as the two men, friends since high school, enjoyed palling around together again after three years. Will bemoaned his friend's status as husband and new father, and would occasionally slip into some venomous diatribe about his friend's wife. I waited for the bus.

An orange hatchback slowed down in front of me, though there wasn't a stoplight or any traffic. I'd grown accustomed to men in cars taking a longer look, and it felt so heavy most of the time that I breathed relief whenever they moved on instead of exposing themselves or leering and saying something inappropriate or predatory—which they did just about every fucking chance they got. I took a mental inventory of what I was wearing having heard that this drag was prone to prostitution. I didn't look sixteen, and had once gotten into a bar with my boss for a night of drinking and dancing, to the dismay of one particular fellow, an enthusiastic dancer who'd disappeared in a hurry after I'd told him I was still in high school. I hoped my white linen capris with their Caribbean blue stripe and my butter yellow tank top didn't scream working girl.

The orange hatchback turned and parked around the corner on a side street, and a guy stepped out, holding on to the car's door.

"Hey, you need a ride?" he asked.

I got up from the bus bench and walked over. He had a sincere face and a crooked smile, and he looked almost embarrassed. He had curly reddish brown hair trimmed neatly at his neck, and a well shaped beard. He was as tall and lean as Danny.

He said. "I'm sorry, I don't know you, but I'm heading down toward the mall."

"I'm not really going anywhere." I said, and walked closer. "I—"

"Well get in, we can find something to do."

We sat across from each other drinking coffee, which he called "mud," in a window booth with a view of Portland's eastside debauchery drag. His name was Cary, and his dark green eyes and everyman demeanor made me forget about Danny. I told him I was from California, and he told me he was a mechanic by trade. The conversation never came around to my age, and his seemed irrelevant.

A couple weeks later, I was thinking about Cary when Danny called. Will had gotten hired on in a strip mall garden center after fabricating his work history at a company that had folded and couldn't be reached for employment verification. He'd be gone most of the afternoon.

"Sheryl said ya' ran off again." He sounded surprised, and I was annoyed that he made it sound like I had so much free will.

"I came to Portland with my uncle."

"Your uncle?"

"Not the uncle that kicked me out."

"Oh, okay."

We talked about nothing in particular, but the entire message was that he was apologetic and taking some kind of arrogant credit for my distance. Maybe he was fishing for some assurance I wasn't pregnant. Or maybe not. Maybe he really was sorry I'd left. Whatever his motivations, it didn't matter, Cary was going to pick me up when he got off work and take me to meet some friends.

***

We were in the darkness of his studio apartment, sobering up and giggling about his buddy, with whom we'd earlier been drinking beer and playing foosball.

"I went to high school with Tony," Cary explained.

"I thought he was going to fall over!" I said. Goofy Tony had been pretty buzzed when we got there, and by the time we left, he was tilting to port, something

Cary said he'd always done. The lanky blonde machinist had a hereditary problem with his left knee, causing it to lock and unlock irregularly, so he often left it unlocked.

"Yeah," Cary said as our chortling dissipated, "he called himself the slack-kneed Swede when I met him."

I didn't know what to say to that, and I felt bad for laughing at him.

"Is he Swedish?" I asked.

Cary snorted, "I don't think so, no!" and we both broke out in belly laughs that shook his bed.

He rolled my way and reached across me. "I'll probably get an earful tomorrow. The couple who lives below me seems to hear everything." His apartment was the upstairs portion of a pretty nice old house, and he told me that the wife often made comments after he had company.

"We weren't exactly being quiet earlier." I mentioned, pointing out to him that his headboard didn't seem to be attached to anything.

He grinned his slanted grin and laid back down.

After a moment of silence, he said, "I just realized we've been out a few times, and I still don't know how old you are."

"I'll be seventeen in August." I said it with pride. I'd gotten used to the looks of disbelief, and there was no point lying to him. He didn't react, so I switched gears. "I like your apartment... except for the bitchy downstairs neighbor." I said.

"Oh, she's nice. It's just an old house," he answered. "I'm moving to Milwaukie anyway."

"What?!" I asked. I was getting tired of people leaving. I'd had enough of it over the last few years. And this news seemed insensitively timed, being dropped during the afterglow portion of our third date. I was vexed, and I didn't hide it, though I'd borne it quietly in most previous cases. "When?" I asked. I wanted to know how long before I had to make another round of good-byes.

"End of the month," he said.

I'd been at ease with our candor with each other on the previous date when he'd told me that he'd been charged with DUI, and I'd told him about bouncing around from home to home. We'd talked about a lot of things that particular night, sneaking around in the late night woods near one of the city's water reservoirs. It seemed that two people who didn't know how to keep secrets had found each other. I didn't know why he'd kept this from me.

"Where is that?" I asked, picturing a quaint logging town, or a sleepy rural community, and hoping there might be a visit to such a place in my future.

"It's about twenty minutes south of here."

"Oohhh."

"What?" he asked. "Did you think I meant—?" he chuckled. "My new apartment is closer to work."

★★★

Cary's dad drove an old green pick-up just like the one Will and I had driven up in. The three of us packed boxes, books, bed parts, and lamps into that truck and moved Cary into a two-bedroom apartment in a quiet complex on a sunny afternoon.

He came in from seeing his dad off red-faced, but happy. "My dad said we should come over for dinner in a couple weeks." I was taking things out of boxes but I had no idea where he wanted stuff, and I didn't feel like I knew him well enough to be pawing through his worldly possessions. "When my brother and his girlfriend are out of town," he specified. I said I'd love to have dinner with his folks.

Cary and I were alone in the apartment the first two nights before his roommate moved in. There was a tavern across from the tune-up shop where he worked, a place to get cold pints after clocking out. Cary and one of his co-workers guzzled with another guy who was a lot attendant at one of the used car dealerships on the strip, and he'd signed on to be Cary's roommate.

The apartment was on the ground floor and the living room had a glass slider out to a concrete patio abbreviated by a chain link fence. Had there been anything other than undeveloped wooded acreage on the other side of the chain link, I would have considered it shabby. As it was, the quiet woods and the shade from the canopy made me fond of the area outside the back door of that apartment, despite the fence. I preferred it to the world outside the front door.

I heard Cary smashing something in the kitchen and went in to survey they wreckage. He was banging his fist down on to a couple packets of ramen, being careful not to rupture the packages.

"What are you doing?" I asked.

"Making dinner." He grinned at me and continued smashing without interruption. "This is the only way to make ramen," he assured me.

It was a Saturday night, and we drank beer with our dinner and well into the night. I told him about my twin uncles, how they were about as similar as marmalade and meatballs. He'd met Will, and they seemed to get along fine. In fact, Will had told me at first that I couldn't spend the night with Cary, then recanted. I expect his reasoning had something to do with safety where drinking and driving were involved.

We drank a lot of beer, and Cary smoked some weed. We enjoyed the draft through the sliding door. The woods outside were pure darkness and it seemed like the fence wasn't even there. I knew those woods were watching us and I loved that.

He plopped down next to me on the sofa with a fresh beer and said, "I should probably tell you what happened the night my brother and me got into that fight."

"Yeah, you said you and him don't speak."

He lit a cigarette. "I was staying there, at my parents' place. You remember. We drove by it the other day, the house with the roses."

"Yeah, I remember." I said. "You said your brother was home, or we would have gone in to say 'hi.'"

"Right. He and his girlfriend Lorna live in the basement living space. Well, they were staying there same time I was." He took a long pull of cheap beer. "I came home late one night. I was pretty drunk, and I was locked out." He poured the remaining half of the beer down his throat, the bottle still chilly and sweating in his hand.

"It was really late, and I remember her letting me in the back door." He jumped up and it startled me. I couldn't figure what he was trying to say. He strode into the kitchen and emerged with two beers this time. He twisted one open and set the second one on the coffee table, returning to his seat and not looking at me.

"Lorna came up and let me in, and I remember us laughing about something." Now he looked at me. "We were in the kitchen laughing, and she was wearing... I guess a long t-shirt." He explained. "She'd been sleeping, I think." He looked at the darkened glass door, shuffled in his seat, then looked down at his beer label. "Well, I guess I went up to my room." He looked at me again. "I was really fucked up. The next thing I remember was being in the dark basement bedroom with her and hearing the TV on in the next room. The basement has two separate rooms."

"Okay."

He hesitated, trying to piece it together. "He was asleep on the couch in the living room, then I was heading up the basement stairs."

We sat in silence. His confession was endearing. I needed Cary to be the real deal, a good guy. I wanted to blame her for wearing nothing but a t-shirt. I searched for anything against the growing disappointment that he too might be just another member of the league of extraordinary opportunists, misogynists, and general jackasses. It was hard to ignore that Cary was responsible for his actions, not Lorna. But I would ignore it.

He continued, "I was hammered, and I guess I got in bed with her, and she though I was him. Jesus, my brother came up swinging. My mom and dad woke up. My mom said I had to get out."

I looked at him, and I thought he might cry. He'd always been jovial, a smartass even. He liked to pull my leg, tell me something absurd and see how far he could string me along. It was always in good fun, never mean-spirited. This was certainly not him pulling my leg. About this, he looked defeated, and I wanted him to feel better.

✦✦✦

"We gotta go camping next weekend, Friday's payday." It was 5:47am on a Sunday, and we'd been up all night. Cary and I were in Will's back yard pulling blackberries off the vines and popping them into our chattery mouths. The night had been fantastic; we'd spent most of the evening at a park with some of Cary's friends, sitting on car hoods and tailgates, or leaning on fenders drinking, then ended up at his apartment. We played cards and drank beer in the living room. Billy, the roommate, emerged for a pee, then slammed his bedroom door around 5am and we discerned that he was displeased with us.

"I've got some business to take care of, anyway," Cary said as we gathered up our things and left the apartment. His plan was to take me to my uncle's, run his errand, then pick me up later.

The June early morning overcast was the most beautiful thing I'd ever seen aside from the grass under our feet, the rose bushes, and the berry vines. Even the tool shed looked like an oil painting. I was uber-sentient like the vibration of a hum that transitions into a melodic note. Cary and I hugged and kissed as our already hammering hearts stipulated. He broke free and left without telling me what his errand was, or when he'd be back. I didn't care. I was thrilled to just be floating around the backyard before slipping into the house, trying not to disturb Will. It was a divine morning.

Cary never came back that day. He called that afternoon, and we got a chuckle out of the fact that we'd both fallen asleep. We both had to work during that week, and we prepared for the next weekend's camping trip.

We had Cary's hatchback loaded to the louvers with gear and beer, and headed out Friday afternoon to a logging town east of Portland. He'd clocked out early—basically the moment his boss slipped his paycheck into his greasy paw, the way he told it—and we were on the road with only one stop to make, he told me. I was surprised when he pulled into the gravel driveway of his parents' house, but relieved that ours was the only vehicle there.

"Stay here," he said, and exited, leaving the car door open. He dashed in the back door.

A few minutes passed, more than I was comfortable with, and I was afraid someone would pull in behind us, or aside the car blocking Cary's door-to-door departure. I knew it wasn't a life or death thing, but who wants a confrontation?

A few more minutes passed and a truck came from up the street and crossed the front of the house. It pulled around one more corner, the corner the house was situated on, and slowed behind me. I froze. It pulled into the gravel driveway right next to me, the driveway belonging to the house next door. I breathed and watched the driver get out, saluting me through chain link, and I half smiled at him. I looked back at the kitchen door of the little green house, and Cary was still not in sight. I looked back at the gear loaded in the back of the car and heard the 'slam' of the screen door. Cary was loping across the walkway with a sawed-off shotgun. He ducked into the car and tucked the gun into the backseat among the sleeping bags. He was giddy. He started the car and put it in reverse. We departed spraying some loose gravel.

"I loaned these to my brother last year. This was about the only fuckin' way I was gonna get 'em back." He smiled at me at a stop sign, and leaned forward reaching into the small of his back. "Open the glove-box," he said.

I did, and he deposited a small handgun inside.

"I'll teach ya' how to shoot." We took off down the avenue and he turned up a Queen song on the radio.

In the Mt. Hood National Forest, service roads snake away from the main highway along rivers, creeks, and trickles, and rebels, rednecks, and horny teens make camp spots just off the roadside. Or is it horny red-necks and rebellious teens? Either way, we set up in a good one along a creek. Nightfall comes prematurely in a gully under thick doug firs; Cary made a fire as tall as he was. The night was clear and chilly at this elevation but we made it work in the tent with our sparse gear.

Saturday morning turned into a more than satisfactory summer afternoon and we rock-hopped to a spot in the creek that was deep enough to swim and cavort in. There were very few others around, but there was a good chance we'd wandered into another campsite's creek shore. There was no way to know for certain that we were totally alone so we tried to be discreet. Even so, I'm sure it was obvious what we were doing as we leaned against the smooth side of a boulder.

At our campsite we drank beer cooled in the creek, and he showed me how the shotgun worked. On the opposite shore of the rocky creek bed was an almost straight-up slope, no access to speak of, no campers or anything. He said we could shoot across safely aiming for things like branches or burls. I was fascinated. I'd never handled a gun before. Even Judd hadn't had any firearms. He'd showed me how to make a pipe bomb, but that was it.

The gun was awkward to hold. I thought I should hold it with one hand like Mad Max, but it was too heavy. I took aim at some cedar branches and squeezed the trigger. Nothing much happened. I don't know what I expected. I guess I thought I'd see some destruction—maybe some splintered branches. I took another shot, this time at something glinting, and it jumped out of view. I couldn't tell what it was.

"You hit it!" Cary said, and set out to cross the creek. He tromped around on the opposite bank for a while then set a can on a snag. I found myself bored with target practice, and stretched out on a towel in the dapple. The negative space above me was in the shape of an ankh where the foliage edged the blue of the sky. If I cocked my head it looked different, more like a figure in a hooded robe. Cary took a shot, and I continued to study the blue. It was as close to perfect of an afternoon as you could get, aside from the intermittent gunshots.

"Hol-lee shit! Look at this." Cary was coming toward me. He showed me the handgun. "I took that shot but it didn't hit anything. But there was no way I could have missed that can, look at it."

I looked across the creek and he was right, that can was a pretty good target. The creek wasn't very wide.

"But look at this." He showed me the end of the barrel where a little .22 round was just poking out and slightly cock-eyed. "If I'd taken another shot it could have blown my hand off."

"Wow, really?"

"Yeah, that thing is stuck in there." He emptied the gun and tugged at the round. "Yep. This one's out of commission for now."

✱✱✱

Two big rivers meet in a little town near Oregon City. It's rural, it's industrial, it's a sport fisherman's playground, and it's a short trip out of Portland. It's where Cary wanted to buy a house. He was a skilled mechanic, and his boss, the owner of the shop on the boulevard where he'd been working for about a year, appreciated his work. The two men had a pretty good working relationship, even though the boss, the way Cary told it, could be dickish about petty things. Sometimes the guys would have to work through their lunch breaks even though the half hour was automatically deducted from their pay. One of them suggested they knock off early on those days, but the boss wouldn't have it. He'd bitch at the guys about tools not being put away properly, or about customers' personal items being disrespected, typical stuff.

We looked at houses on the weekends, peeking into windows and wandering through back yards of bungalows with 'For Sale' signs poked into the front lawns. I loved the rural wooded settings. They had an Americana feel that was missing in Will's suburban lot. The more we looked, the more I fell in love with the idea of setting up housekeeping.

Cary charmed me with a side trip to the historic district overlooking the river on a Saturday in August just before my seventeenth birthday. We walked along the cliff above the riverfront district and ate convenience store corn dogs at a park picnic bench, washing them down with cans of Hamm's. The river was magnificent, and the breeze in the trees felt like home. That bend in the river seemed to be the higher reason I'd left California. I loved California, but I didn't miss it.

It made sense, now. I'd been running *to* something, not *from*. I wasn't a runaway, I was an itinerant, a seeker, a wayfarer, and now I was home.

That night we stayed in at the apartment and ordered pizza with Billy the roommate. The three of us watched TV in silence. I didn't know Billy at all, and he didn't go out of his way to talk to me. When the pizza box was empty he went into his room without saying a thing to either of us.

We laid in bed giggling and whispering later that night. He told me Billy was a different person than he'd been when they were making plans to rent the apartment. They'd laughed and joked before, at the tavern. Now Billy hardly talked to him, and he had no explanation for the change.

✸✸✸

Cary picked me up at Will's on a Friday after his shift. I'd also worked that day, and we'd made plans to catch up with his sister Beth at a family friend's barbecue. At 7:30 I flip-flopped down the driveway to meet him at his car.

"Let's go!" he said, "they're waitin' for us." He stepped out of the car and hung onto the driver's door and the roof of the car, which was good, because he looked wonky on his own feet.

I stopped short and studied him.

"Come on, baby!" he slurred. "We're not gettin' any younger!"

I shouted back. "I'll be right there, let me get my stuff," and trotted back in for my purse. I didn't want Will to see him.

Down the avenue, he talked about work, and other things. I sat in the passenger seat wishing I could remember how to drive a stick. His head bobbed loose on his shoulders, and he reminded me of my mom those school day afternoons when she was working the night shift at the hotel—those afternoons I'd come home and she'd be talking nonsense among the empties.

"We gotta go by the apartment," he said.

That made me nervous, we were already three-quarters of the way to where I guessed the party was, I didn't know how he was going to be able to drive a further eight miles.

We made it to his place without incident if you don't count his shitty parking job. Once inside, Cary made for the bedroom and rummaged around in his dresser until he'd produced a small wooden box not unlike the one that had traveled with me from the valley to South City, except that his wasn't a puzzle to open. He grinned at me with one eye half closed and held up a plastic baggie of pale beige crystals. "I gotta straighten out."

Out in the living room, I realized the apartment was a mess. He prepared the drug at the coffee table and asked me to get a couple beers. I went to the fridge and found no beer therein. I went back to the living room and sat down next to him, watching him smash... tap-tap-tap out two lines. He looked at me, reaching around for his wallet and smiling. His smile turned when he said, "Beer?"

"There isn't—"

"Shit," He said pressing his wallet against his forehead, "They're in the car."

I took his keys and retrieved a five-plus-one-empty pack from the car and came back to find him leaning forward so he could see me coming in. I plopped the beer box on the sofa between us, and he handed me the rolled twenty. He pulled a bottle making a 'gak!' noise in the back of his throat and shaking his head.

He popped the beer with his lighter, and leaned back on the sofa cushion, "Aah, better."

The speed did straighten him out, but we were in no hurry to leave, and after about an hour we decided not to go to the barbecue at all.

He sat up straight and said, "I need to call my sister. I'll see if she wants to come over here." He got up and grabbed the phone, straightening and leading the cord away from the kitchen table to his sofa spot. He sat back down next to me and dialed, leaning in for a peck while it rang. He was almost perfectly sober.

"Hey man!" he sang. "Lemme talk to Beth." He paused. "Yeah in a bit, I'm just hangin' with my girlfriend right now." He winked at me.

"Hey." he said. "I'm at my apartment with Connie." He grinned big, "We didn't make it that far—why don't you come over here?" The grin fell away. "No, everything's fine. Bring some beer." He hung up.

He hugged me tight and kissed my neck. "Well, we don't have to go anywhere. She's on her way."

✦✦✦

I worked at a pizza place in the mall because of course. It was a shortish bus ride from my uncle's house, and Cary showed up unexpected one night to pick me up. He was parked in the far end of the lot by the bus stop when I walked out. I was happy to see him but wondered why he was there so late on a work night.

He didn't say much except that he'd been at a nearby tavern on the avenue. He drove me home in semi-silence and it became apparent that he was pretty buzzed. I asked him who he'd been with, if he'd talked to his sister or his mom. I questioned him trying to bring him out of the ether but my questions went unanswered. We drove in silence past sickly neon lights, fast food drive-thrus and strip malls. He missed the right turn at Will's street and I asked him where he was going.

"Goddammit!" He gunned it through a yellow light, turned and snaked his way through side streets, stopped, then shot across five lanes to land a block and a half short of my uncle's house. He parked and shut the car off.

"It's been a shit day," he said.

"What happened?"

He flopped his head back and sighed. "Well, first of all, Billy moved out."

"What? When?" I remembered the apartment had looked ransacked the night his sister came over, and there had been a tapestry missing. "Why? It's only been two months."

"Fuck if I know."

He reached to the glove box quickly, startling me. He pulled out his handgun and emptied it. "I need you to keep these tonight, I don't want to be responsible for what might happen if I have them." He held his fist out to me. I opened my hands in my lap and he deposited the brassy rounds into them.

He rubbed his temples.

"You can get another roommate, right?" I didn't know what to say and I looked out my window at the house we were parked in front of, wondering if the occupants knew we were there, if they would be suspicious of strangers parking there at close to midnight. I closed my hand around the bullets.

"I don't know. I don't know shit anymore," he said barely above a whisper. "I can't think. I don't know how it got..."

He looked a thousand yards beyond me, beyond my window and the curb outside it, his head cocked to the side against the car's seatback. He looked like he might weep. Maybe he too thought about the people who lived in that house out there, what their lives were like. Maybe he wished he could be one of them, or maybe he wondered how they would each eventually die. Maybe he wondered how I would die, or how he would. Maybe.

"It's not as bad as it seems right now." I just wanted him to feel better. "It'll all look different in the daytime."

I said more useless and syrupy things, things I'd seen on motivational posters or heard in epilogues of Afterschool Specials. After a while, he looked at me and sighed, cutting off one of my flowery diatribes.

"I just think we all go through it," I offered.

He sat up straight, looked at the gun in his hand and shoved it under the seat. He took another quick glance at me, rubbed the stubble on his cheeks and started the car. I'd closed my hand tight around the shells at some point, and I opened it as he inched down the street to stop in front of my uncle's darkened bungalow. The bullets were almost glued to my palm, and the ones that rolled away revealed indentations in my skin.

He put the car in neutral and pulled the brake. "Whaddya wanna do this weekend?"

I cracked a wide smile when he said that, still looking down at my discolored palm. "Whatever you want to do." I said, looking up at him. He was still dour, even though I'd talked him out of the weeds. He looked at my hand, then at the open glove compartment. I took the cue.

"I'm just going to drop these in here, okay?"

"Yeah, go ahead."

"We'll come up with a plan," I said. "This weekend. Let's go out to the park over the river and think of a plan." He leaned in to shut the glove box and I kissed him. "Okay?"

"Yes, the river," he said, and kissed me back.

I got out of the car and headed up the driveway and he said he'd call me.

★★★

As Will drank screwdrivers and smoked pot with one of his friends I waited for Cary. It was Will's birthday, and I wasn't sure if he was celebrating that, or the fact that he'd just lost his job.

I had talked to Cary twice since the night he drove me home from work, but it was the end of the week, and he was late to pick me up for our weekend gallivant-presumptive. I sat on the front porch slab behind a thick boxwood waiting and thinking as the quarter-hours passed that he might be at the tavern again. I could hear Will and his friend listening to Cab Calloway inside the front door, which was barricaded by a bookshelf in the living room. Will only used the side door, leaving the front door unanswered to strangers, salesmen, and bill collectors.

I went inside and Will made a show of my appearance. "Hey," he said to his drinking buddy, "can you believe she's only seventeen?" His friend seemed uncomfortable, but it never bothered me, I took it as a compliment. The tendency to adultize me, however subtly, would be a convenient and destructive tool, especially given my own participation in it.

I shouted an inquiry over "You're Nobody Till Somebody Loves You" to find out that Cary hadn't called. I asked Will if he would mind passing on a message then headed out to catch a bus. The tavern was just a few stops before the mall where I worked, and less than ten blocks from Cary's parents' house.

His hatchback wasn't in the parking lot, but I went inside anyway. The sound of a Bad Company song and the smack of pool balls came loud through the smoke and neon. There were plenty of revelers there this Friday night, but Cary wasn't among them. I took a few steps in and to the side toward a pay phone on the wall, scanning the crowd for details—anything that looked like a paused conversation or a half-consumed beer topped by a coaster—in case he was in the men's room. I couldn't linger too long lest the bartender make me for a minor, and I slipped out satisfied he wasn't there.

I walked over to his parents' house. The neighborhood was quiet once you got off the drag and away from the tavern. There were many gravel driveways, nautical pilings and dock ropes adorning flowerbeds, hand-crafted mailboxes, and other charming bits of folksy ephemera at these homes. This neighborhood didn't have sidewalks, the lawns just ended where the blacktop started unless the homeowner had installed some landscaping, usually planted out with barberry, Oregon grape, azalea, or some other such native shrubbery. I stopped across the street from Cary's folks' hunter green house with the white trim and stared, feeling left out, conspired against. I wanted to knock. His car wasn't there, but I wanted to inquire. Lights were on, but I felt like a bother, like an intruder, or like a pest. I felt abandoned. I headed back to the bus.

A white Chevy S-10 stopped ahead of me, two blocks out of the lights of the avenue. I had to walk around the truck and turn at the stop sign to get to the bus stop. As I approached, he turned off his lights, and as

I walked past his truck I could see that the driver had his dick in his hand.

I waited for the bus in front of a tiny Chinese food restaurant, across from a convenience store. I felt prone as the cars whipped past, and stared at when the traffic was stopped at a red. I was probably paranoid, but I was suddenly quite aware that I was wearing cut-off denim shorts and a tight t-shirt, summer night or not. I hoped I would find Cary at Will's when I got back. I figured he would dig Cab Calloway. But I also had a feeling I would not find him there. He was somewhere else, somewhere I would not be able to find him tonight, I felt that. It was most likely that he—

A Portland Police cruiser made a quickie right turn directly in front of me, and stopped in the Chinese restaurant's parking lot, blocking the walkway to the door, and lit up its red-blues.

The sedan's dirty white doors flipped open and a pair of officers stepped out, both male and with a decent age difference between them. They asked me questions, one writing on a small pad, the other leaning an arm on his belt. I told them exactly who I was, what I'd been doing, and where I was headed. I felt suddenly clothed in the shorts and t-shirt of shame.

The younger officer returned to the car while the other one gave me a grandfatherly lecture about young girls and whatever-the-fuck boogeyman of the day is most effective at deflecting mortal man's responsibility for the mistreatment of said young girls. I didn't have a criminal record, and I'd done nothing wrong, so I wasn't worried. He finished up with a "Get on home, young lady," when he got the high sign from his partner, and the timing couldn't have been better. The bus was stopped at the red light, door open.

I sat at the back of the bus and planned to call Cary in the morning. I went over all the possibilities of where he could be. I kept coming back to the picture in my head that he was passed out drunk at his apartment, because that was my favorite explanation for his absence. About a mile and a half up the bus pulled over where there wasn't a stop and the driver said, "Just a moment, folks." About two seconds before I saw the red-blue flashes outside the bus, I had a feeling I was the reason we were stopped, and about 2.8 seconds after that, my two officers appeared, the young one standing by the back door and grandfather coming in the front, hand hanging near one of the many things on his belt.

The ride was short. They told me my name had come up as a runaway from California, naturally. I started to sob the moment I realized I'd be sent back. The older officer asked my why I was crying and I told him I was afraid of losing my job. The rookie asked me why I'd given them a phony name, and the question confused me. I said I didn't, he insisted I did. The accusation seemed senseless, and it was intimidating. I've never understood what had he to gain by accusing me of something we both knew didn't happen, unless it was to get me to stop crying, which it did.

Chapter Eight: House of Doors

*A*s a ward of the State of California—a status I didn't know existed up to that point—I was processed into a group home. Since the officers had plucked me off the bus I'd spent a few days in a juvenile detention center, before being escorted onto a plane, picked up by a social worker at the airport, then chauffeured to my new address in San Francisco's Richmond district right around supper time. I was quartered with another girl in a big room in a very nice Victorian three-story. I told her about my situation, and she told me about the kitchen rules. There were three boys in the house; one was just a kid at twelve, the other two were our age. We were non-violent displaced youths—throw-away kids. We were the charges of strangers who were state employees. For some of us, it may have been a better home than that from which we'd drifted or been ejected.

We heeded the rules and curfews, and treated the counselors with the same respect they offered us. The girl I roomed with had a job and was gone all day on my second full day there. I spent most of the day in the basement of the house with one of the other boys, watching him hit balls around on the worn out pool table and listening to him talk about his extended family like they were here instead of across the bay in Oakland. Raymond was his name and he was one of the easiest guys to be around I'd ever met, and a terrible shot with a pool cue. He was a big bear of a boy with a soft, deep voice. The other kid barely spoke to anyone, except for Raymond, and only when it was just the two of them. I could hear them bullshitting in their room at night in jubilant Ebonics like they'd been best friends since childhood, even though they'd only met when Raymond came to the house in June.

On the third day, after having earned some free time, I took the bus to North Beach to hunt down my mom, an activity that usually involved stopping into one of three or four bars, or standing on the sidewalk outside a deli on and shouting "MOM!" at a chubby cartoon butcher on a Plexiglas sign. She shared a single room in a residence hotel with a man called Ducky, and their room's only window was behind the deli's sign. If the window was open, and she was in the room, shouting usually worked out. I'd gained this experience by occasionally sneaking up to the city on the train when I was living with Lawrence. I would visit with my mom or have lunch, usually telling him I was shopping with Sheryl or Alice. Today she wasn't in her room, and neither was Ducky. A bartender at the café around the corner told me she was clerking at the Unitarian Church and told me which bus to take to get there.

She wasn't surprised to see me. Will had called her while I was in juvie. When he came to visit, I'd told him I'd seen an airline ticket on the office desk when I'd requested access to my birth control pills—a ticket to San Francisco with my name on it. I don't know why they shipped me back to within three miles of my mom, but it didn't matter. I went to her because I needed a bus ticket back to Portland.

I spent the afternoon in the office of the Unitarian Church helping her make some copies on an old mimeograph machine. At the end of her workday I ate a cup of yogurt she'd given me from the break room refrigerator while she washed the office's dishes, saying that if she didn't do it, nobody else would.

On our way out of the church, as she checked out with her co-workers, I looked around the nave, trying to glean clues on who the Unitarians were. There was a lot of very polished wood, some cheap-ish looking appointments, like they'd been cobbled together from thrift stores and sidewalk sales, and modern design in the stained glass windows. I even thought about the word, "Unitarian" and hoped it meant folks of different faiths united in their worship, a sort of Happy Hippie Christianity.

We walked out into the city sunshine and she confirmed my plans. "So, you want to go back to Portland, huh?"

"Yeah," I said. "I have a job there."

"Does Will want you to come back?"

"Yeah."

We stopped in the sunshine, and she looked at me. "Will says you have a boyfriend?"

"Yeah, Cary," I said.

"And is he older than you."

"Yeah, a little," I confirmed.

"This way." She pointed up an alley and we started walking again. "We'll walk up here to the bank and I'll get you some cash."

"You should come for a visit, you'd like him."

"Is he a nice guy, does he treat you right?" she asked.

"Oh yeah, he's awesome," I said, missing him.

"I'm glad, honey. But don't forget, you've only known him a couple months." She stopped to catch her breath on the alley's stair-stepped sidewalk. "I was with Ted for almost ten years before realizing what a creep he was," she said, looking up to the next street.

"I know, but Cary's not like Ted," I said. "Besides, I'm not planning to marry him." The thought of this made me giggle.

"I'm sure he's not." She smiled, and I knew she was sincere and wouldn't push the matter any further. We continued up the hill to the bank machine at the corner. "I'll come up to Portland soon, I wouldn't mind getting out of the city."

She gave me some money and directions to the bus station from the group home. My plan was to leave the following morning. I had to be back at the house by supper. I was burning through the free time I'd earned from cleaning the kitchen after the youngest boy had begged off his duty for reasons unexplained. She walked with me to catch the bus back to the group home and we hugged goodbye. She again promised to come for a visit soon.

At the home, I found Raymond in the basement with Mr. Quiet, who exited as soon as I came down. I told him I was leaving and he looked puzzled, even asked why I would want to leave there. I picked up a pool cue and took a couple shots while I explained what I was missing in up north. He listened, and I realized that until now, he'd always done the majority of the talking. He asked if my boyfriend was white. I didn't tell him my mom gave me money, but he told me not to tell anyone in the house that I had cash. One of the counselors came down and chatted us up as we, not so much played a game of pool, as just shot at balls that looked vulnerable. It was getting near quiet time, and the counselor, a bearded olive-skinned fellow in his forties walked with me upstairs telling me that they'd found a foster home they thought would be a good match for me, and that the mother was going to come by around lunch time the following day to pick me up.

It wasn't good news. I wouldn't have a chance to earn any more free time unless someone missed their breakfast clean-up. Our bedroom window was barred, and the stairs and landing creaked like you might expect an old Victorian house to creak. The counselor sensed my stress, furrowed his brow, and started to ask if I was okay, but I cut him off.

"Where's the foster home?" I blurted.

"They live in Concord. Why?"

"Okay. No reason."

I trotted up those damn creaky stairs eager to get into my room and sort out exactly how I was going to make my escape as he bid 'goodnight' to my back.

I closed the door and flung myself onto the twin bed without even bothering to turn on a light. My bunkie wasn't home, working the late shift, I guessed. I realized I might have to delay my trip back north depending on how attentive my new foster-mother was. I remembered how hard it was to get out of Shelly's rifle-scope. And, I'd have to take the Greyhound from Concord, except that I didn't know where the station was in Concord. It had been exactly a week since I'd gone out to look for Cary and been spirited away. I didn't want to wait another week, and I certainly didn't want to try to hang onto my traveling money in another foster home. I had to sleep *some* time.

When I woke in the morning, the other bed still looked un-slept in. I went down to the office and found a counselor on duty that I hadn't met yet, a waifish blonde who looked like she couldn't have been much more than a teen herself. The Pixie counselor asked me if I'd seen my roommate and I told her I hadn't, glancing at the blackboard where we signed up for chores.

"I'll clean up after breakfast if she doesn't," I said.

Pixie shot me a look, and I chalked my name in on the board under my roommate's. I needed to earn the free time, and I could cash it in just after the dishes were done and be on a bus by the time the foster-mom from Concord showed up. I was sure there was a bus out before the lunch hour.

Over pancakes, Pixie asked me if I knew anything about my bunkie's whereabouts; if she'd told me she was going to run, or if she'd planned any activities after work. I didn't know anything. I'd barely spoken to her as I was making plans of my own. The boys were no help either. She sighed and went over her shift's to-do list out loud, including transfer paperwork on me, and missing resident paperwork on my roommate if she didn't show up by the time the next counselor came on.

I hustled the cleanup after breakfast and flew up to my room to get dressed and pack. I could only take what I could fit in an oversized purse. I couldn't walk out with the duffel bag I'd come with. The hideous but useful purse I planned to use had been left behind by another girl who'd stayed in that room. My now missing roommate had already told me she didn't want it. Luck was with me. I fished through the pile of clothes on the closet floor she called her wardrobe. We'd admired each other's things, and even though she had a lot more that I did, she was fond of one of my items—a charcoal grey leather, steel-studded belt. I found it in the pile and began to roll it up to fit in my bag but decided to leave it there for her. A parting gift.

Sitting at the make-up table in our room a small knock came at the door. Pixie counselor poked her head in with an update.

"So… the lady from Concord says she'd like to come by around 12:30." She was semi-asking. "Does that work for you?"

"Um, I guess," I said.

She stepped into the room. "Lemme put it another way, we can't hold you here," she said. "If you have other plans I'll tell her not to come. Let's not make her make the trip for nothing."

"Oh," I said, trying on this new candor to see how it fit. "Yeah, I won't be here."

"Okay, I'll let her know," she said, and gave me a smile.

It surprised me that I had some measure of free will, and I gave it some thought, but I was sure I didn't belong with the family in Concord. If it was a 'good' family, they'd figure out sooner or later that I was of no value and send me on my way, and if it was another Judd and Shelly...

I repacked everything but the belt into my duffel bag and went to the basement to say goodbye to Raymond. He was there with the other two boys clanking the pool balls together without using cues, curling their hands over whichever colored ball pleased them and laughing when the balls bounced around in a violent jangle. They'd made quite a chaotic game of it, sometimes even sinking one. He smiled when he saw my bag, maybe expressing a final approval of my decision. We hugged and he wished me peace. Before I could go out the basement's exterior door, the twelve-year-old ran up on me and gave me a tight hug around the hips, then scurried away up the back stairs. All I could do was watch him run off while Raymond shrugged.

***

Will picked me up at the Greyhound station in Portland early the next morning and issued a terse diatribe about our living situation version two-point-oh. He reminded me that I'd have to work and go to school. That was my plan too, but I doubted I'd get my job at the mall back. And we'd talked about school before but were both stymied as to how to get me back in. He'd said he would not assume legal guardianship of me because he didn't want the state poking its nose into his personal life. As far as I knew I couldn't get my school records without a guardian. I had about a month to come up with a plan.

I slept most of that day, and called Cary in the evening. He was unnecessarily apologetic and we made plans to get together immediately. I told him I'd take the bus to his apartment and meet him after work.

I woke up exhausted, and with a headache. I suffered the bus ride to his apartment and let myself in to wait. The apartment was still a mess but I had no energy to clean up. The thirteen-hour bus trip had left me fatigued. He found me curled up in his bed when he got home, and settled in next to me. We relaxed there and talked for a long while; I told him about San Francisco, and he told me he'd been at Tony's the night I couldn't find him. He'd had entirely too much to drink by 7:00 that evening, by 8:30 Tony had taken his keys, and by 9:30, a little after I was booked into the detention center, he was passed out. He said, in his charming way, that he would take suggestions for how he could make it up to me, and his off-center grin pried a pathetic chuckle out of me.

By the end of the week it was clear I was sick. Cary had originally assumed I had a cold, but after a few days, he suggested I might have a sinus infection and took me to a nearby clinic. After asking me if I'd recently been traveling, a physician's assistant agreed to Cary's diagnosis and prescribed a course of antibiotics that would last well beyond the disappearance of the symptoms. I'd spent most of the week at Cary's and

Will didn't seem to mind. When I got back to his place, I gave him the good news that I'd called in to the mall and gotten my job at the pizza place back.

I worked my first couple scheduled shifts commuting from Will's, then headed back out to Cary's to find him wrecked; sober and defeated.

He was sitting at one of the kitchen chairs hunched over and surrounded by clutter, his head hanging between his shoulders. "There's something I didn't tell you when you came back," he said.

I was reminded of the night I held those bullets in my hand—he looked *that* lost. I felt wobbly on my knees standing there at that moment and wondering where those bullets were now.

"Me and my buddy Dan walked off the job," he said.

I stood there. "What do you mean?"

He looked up at me. "While you were gone."

I looked at him and could only blink and shake my head.

"We walked off to teach that asshole a lesson." He waved an arm for dramatic effect. "He acts like we're not important to his business. We are his business!"

"Yeah?" I said, still not getting where he was going with this.

"Well, so, okay. We were out of work for a few days. But he called us back and apologized. Everything's cool, right?"

"Umm... wrong?" I fished.

"Yeah, that Greek son of a bitch is now sayin' my raise is another six months out since I'm now technically a new hire."

I was catching on. "What the fuck?!"

"Exactly," Cary agreed. "The problem is, I lost almost a week's pay, and I've got rent comin' due... and no roommate. It was hard enough covering August after Billy skedaddled without saying anything."

There was nothing I could do or say. I was only working part time at minimum wage.

"I've got five days to come up with rent and then some. There's no way."

His held his head in his hands and sighed. There was only one thing I could do to make him feel better—a diversion, but better than standing there helpless.

His distress didn't stop him from participating with enthusiasm in the distraction I'd offered, until we both slipped into a deep sleep having skipped dinner. I dreamed there was someone outside the apartment, by the windows, skulking around the front door. I dreamed there was a tapping on the sliding glass but no figure outside. I woke up in a panic. I thought something was coming for me, coming to drag me away. Again. Still. I sat up in the darkness and listened to hear absolutely nothing. He didn't wake up, and his sound sleep was a comfort to me and I lied awake for a while just listening to him sleep. Cary left for work in the morning still sullen, but a little less shaken.

I told Will that afternoon about Cary's predicament, starting with the story of the workplace walk-out. He chuckled, saying I had a knack for picking deadbeats. He quickly elevated his own status with bit of news. "I just interviewed at the gas station on the corner by the grocery store, by the way. They need someone on graveyard. Hopefully the guy will call in the next couple days."

"Yeah, that'd be cool," I said, even though I couldn't picture my uncle pumping gas on the graveyard shift.

He loaded a bowl and said, "I didn't know Cary was union," as he tapped the lighter on the kitchen table. He lit the pipe.

"He's not," I said.

He nodded in confirmation holding in a deep marijuana hit. He held the pipe and lighter out to me and cocked an eyebrow.

"No thanks, I'm good," I said.

He shrugged and exhaled, and I breathed in the sweet, thick smoke.

"You know," he said, "he can crash here."

"Really!?" I said.

"Isn't that what you were going to ask?"

"Well, I thought about it, but I didn't think you'd like the idea."

"He can have the basement for $150 a month, just as long as you two can behave yourselves," he said, leaving the interpretation therof somewhat open.

"Oh gawd, this is going to be such a relief for him!" I gushed.

✹✹✹

Will's basement had a shower, the laundry, and a section that was partially finished that had served as a summertime bedroom for the previous owners. I had assumed that Will wouldn't let us sleep in the same room, but it didn't matter once he started working nights at the gas station. All summer, my twin mattress had been in the attic room that seemed to stay cool enough as long as I left the windows open at either end, and kept a fan running. But the first week of September served up a couple of unbearably hot evenings, and we were glad to have Cary's bed in the basement and the nights to ourselves.

We sprawled in cool-ish comfort on a quiet week-night and Cary told me he still wanted to buy a house. I hadn't thought in those terms in weeks, and I was sure he would have put the idea out of his head after moving twice in one summer, not to mention how badly his little workers' strike had backfired. We were surrounded by boxes of his things; his alarm clock was on a moving box, his dresser was essentially a series of boxes and a suitcase—and I thought 'how convenient.' But for the moment he was happy, which made me happy.

Will didn't bring up me going to school again, probably because he knew that as long as he refused to assume guardianship of me, there was nothing that could be done. He was content to ignore the situation until a solution presented itself, and he was eager not to invite any state authorities into his life. He batted around the idea of starting a small illegal horticultural enterprise in a corner of the basement. I had some ideas of my own; applying for emancipation, getting my GED, going to an alternative school. But I figured the paperwork on any of those things would likely outlast the eleven months it would take me to turn eighteen. So I was content to make pizzas at the mall and be Cary's girlfriend.

✦✦✦

In short order, we got back up to spending time with his friends on weekends and once in a while during the week. It's hard to resist the urge to squeeze every last droplet of joie de vivre out of the summer months in Portland. And we did. At first we were simply timing our arrivals home in the evening so as not to disturb Will while he was getting off to work. It made for the occasional late work night for Cary, but the stress he'd been feeling the entire month of August had dissipated.

One warm September night he left me behind. It had been over four hours since he would have clocked out at the tune-up shop. I went from worried to pissed off, then back to worried again.

Will had left for work not realizing anything was wrong. I stayed in the attic room as he got ready to leave, shouting 'goodbye' to him on his way out. I tried to keep the living situation as drama-free as possible.

Cary sometimes went dark—quiet and dark. We would be hanging out with friends, laughing and joking. Then he'd retreat into his own head, hunched up-like, and looking on, no longer part of the group and out of reach. I hadn't seen it since we'd moved in with Will.

I heard him pull up, and I went outside to confront him since I was, by this time, back in the pissed off cycle. He'd been drinking but wasn't drunk. I took this to mean he'd 'straightened out,' and it seemed he'd landed in a mood. The way he looked at me I knew he was unreachable, and right away it was clear he intended to spend the night elsewhere. I'd never seen him quite like this, nor would I have guessed this much fury could have been contained in the heart of a man who'd once playfully teased me about what became of the rest of the potato after a jo-jo wedge was cut. He raged into the house and down to the basement, rifling through the boxes that contained his clothes. I responded to his aggravation with the skill of a scorned teenage girl. I threw accusations and gasoline. I denied him approval. He picked up his alarm clock to get inside the box it was on, stood up straight pausing, and smashed the clock to the concrete floor. I took a step back and he strode up the stairs to the back door, cursing. I followed.

He stormed out to his car, and I went up to the second floor attic room. I stood, arms crossed, at the window that overlooked the driveway. I could hear him complaining and slamming his car's hatchback, then the door. He shuffled back up the driveway, grumbling something I couldn't make out. I backed away from the window just in time to hear a single gunshot. It wasn't like you hear in the movies. It was thin and popcorn-y. For a moment I was afraid. Only a moment. It took that pea-sized pebble of Earth's time for me to think about what he might do—whether or not he would come in the house and up the stairs, gun in hand—then I worried about his safety instead of mine. I stood in the dim vaulted room away from the window, and I heard a sound I didn't recognize, a thud. I flew down the stairs and out to the driveway and stood there in my socks. The unbearably hot nights had given way to bright September coolness. He was in the driver's seat, head down, fiddling with something under the dome light. I couldn't stop him if he wanted to leave, I knew that, and I didn't want to make the situation worse. We'd never talked to each other like that before. I wanted to put the gasoline back in the can. I wanted to back up and meet his frustration with understanding. I turned to go back into the house when a short bleat of the car's horn drew my attention back. I turned and saw that he had the small gun to his right temple. His eyes were fixed on me through the windshield with the same chemically imbalanced fury I'd seen twenty minutes before. Another tinny shot came and his head fell back and his hand dropped into his lap.

A few weeks later, Cary's sister and I sat in his old room in his parents' house listening to the rest of the family downstairs. The room was empty except for the two of us sitting on the floor leaning up against one wall. Beth told me some story or other about she and Cary as kids. We could hear her niece downstairs, and she marveled at the size of her family, then she went quiet. After a few minutes she confided in me that she'd recently had a miscarriage, to the disappointment of her and her fiancé. It was too much heartbreak for one woman.

I had something to tell, too, and I would have shared it with her even if she hadn't said what she'd said. When she was quiet again, and we could hear that it was also quiet downstairs, I told her I was pretty sure I was pregnant.

★★★

San Jose was hot and smoggy as Will and I loaded into Elyse's SUV at the airport curb. Upon arrival, Gram briefed us on the mishmash of information she'd gotten out of belligerent Bob about the circumstances of my mom's death. Bob was her new boyfriend, and not near as easy to talk to as Ducky had been. It was my job to get the rest of the story out of him. I dialed the number she'd given Gram and got no answer, and I promised I'd try again after a nap. I didn't bother telling her I needed to dispose of the worst hangover I could recently remember.

I shut myself in the guest room, laying on the sofa with a throw pillow over one ear, peeking up at snap-shots on the bookcase of people who may as well have been strangers. Elyse, the twins, my mom, even my other two uncles, all in their twenties or so, and all only vaguely recognizable, except that they all looked like each other. I had a few pictures of my son and he looked like me, but with Cary's eyes, not like these people. It was the pictures Beth had occasionally sent me that I'd used as inspiration for my drawings, and when I got his adorable little freckled face just right, he didn't look like me or like anyone else in that family. He looked like the broad-shouldered super-hero boy he was.

I hoped then, more than I ever had before that I could meet him someday, if Beth didn't mind.

✱✱✱

Bob explained to me that they'd been in Key West since the end of April, and she'd been very 'sick.' The reality was she'd committed slow suicide, drinking herself, over the course of two decades, into organ failure. Elyse blamed him, but she'd done it to herself.

He'd been resistant and vague when either she or Gram had tried to talk to him, and Elyse was pissed off about that, too. I got him to agree to gather her things together for our visit the following day.

The four of us drove into the city and collected a box from the front stoop of the apartment she'd shared for about six years with the retired police captain from New Jersey. He was home, he just didn't care to talk to us. Elyse was unimpressed with his callousness and that he wouldn't face us. She had indignant covered. The box was the size of a microwave oven, what was left of my mom's entire life inside. Back at Gram's we examined the contents of the carton. She hadn't much, and that was exactly what he'd left for us. About all she'd had of value was a small collection of jewelry that he'd kept.

✱✱✱

Will and I drove back to the city the following day, but on a different pilgrimage. Over the years, we'd come down from Portland whenever we could to attend Pride weekend in the city with my mom. The three of us were members of an little club in that way; we enjoyed San Francisco's Pride festivities together, the one 'family thing' we did. It would be my mom's final clever bid, to slough off her brittle coil in June so Will and I could find ourselves in the bay area for Gay Pride weekend.

Will drove up the highway out of San Jose, to the interchange that Sheryl's old apartment overlooked. He took the westbound cloverleaf and we traveled a two-lane stretch that traverses a reservoir concealing a fault line, and meanders past a cemetery and a number of farms—chiefly supporting pumpkin fields. Gay Pride promised the utmost festivities and we both knew it, even if neither of us felt all that festive.

Will broke the silence. "Whenever I drive this way I see the signs that say artesians."

I furrowed my brow, for I could not begin to calculate what he'd just said. "Whhhat?" I asked.

"They have shops at some of these farms," he explained, "and some of them say 'artesians' on the sign."

I gave it a moment's thought, then it hit me. "I think you mean artisans," I said.

"Yeah, like that one!" He pointed as we cruised by a farmer's market with fresh produce and handcrafts. "I know, but for the longest time, I though it said artesians."

I knew what he was talking about, and I marveled at the pervasive nature of advertising. Those beer commercials *were* funny, and his misconception just made it more amusing. I snorted.

"Whaaaat?" he asked with a broad smile. "Me and my friends used to come out here a lot. My buddy Champ lives out here."

I giggled even more at the things we misperceive and gloss right over without even questioning. It was silly and he knew it. We laughed again when we passed another farm with a similar sign, noticing that, in this case 'artisans' was misspelled 'artesans' legitimizing his error. It felt great to laugh.

My mom and I had also taken this route many times when I was a girl—before I was twelve, where my best memories of her live. There was a modest house in front of a large escarpment along the highway that my mom adored. On the north side of the road, heading west was the house built entirely out of doors. Usually we just whipped by it, but sometimes when the traffic was heavier, we could take time to look at it. Instead of siding, the builder had fashioned the little cottage's exterior out of nothing but old doors and a few windows. They were different colors and some of the doors had windows of their own, and I loved thinking that instead of all being fixed in place, that maybe random ones functioned, perhaps in an unexpected way. Maybe some of them swiveled, or tipped up, or swung like a saloon door.

She'd shout as we drove by, "Look, Connie, there it is! There's the house of doors!"

We'd moved pretty much every year she was married to Ted, and on one occasion I'd asked her if she'd like to live there, in the house made out of doors. I thought it was the coolest house I'd ever seen and I wanted to live there, and I asked her if we could.

She said, "Sure, why not? I bet we'd be happy living in that house, just me and you."

About the Author

C.L. Herridge is a designer and writer living in Yamhill County, Oregon. She studied graphic design and arts & letters at Portland Community College and Portland State University, respectively. Herridge volunteers with the Arts Alliance of Yamhill County and lives in Oregon's wine and timber region with her husband, a sous chef. She writes fiction, cultivates hops, and dabbles in folk art. Herridge's first novel, *Cascadia Park* is available on Amazon.